THE CARPET BOMB EMPORIUM

Jacob Benedetti

CONTENTS

Welcome to the Carpet Bomb Emporium 1

Today I'm Sick.......... 2

Not too sure about this guy 5

Read the Room 7

Great Ideas 9

Slug 11

Going Shopping 12

Coming to Terms 16

Meeting............. 18

The Sick Sir.......... 19

Checkup #1 23

Church Girl.......... 24

We live in a material world, and I'm a mechanical gorilla tearing out her inner workings to get revenge on her creator............ 25

Animal............... 27

Logic 28

Circus 29

The Day I Froze Time.. 30

The Bird Dream....... 32

Cancer Scare 35

My Pink Eye 36

Point of View from a Cannibal....... 42

Necro............... 44

Open-Heart Surgery for the Caloric Glutton.... 46

Pike 54

Checkup #2.......... 55

Contact High 56

Duck Waddlers 58

Feel the Burn......... 59

Screaming into Sleep... 61

Sweaty Socks......... 64

Dirty Wanker 65	A List of Beverages You Remind Me Of. . . 117
fatso. 67	It Sorta Feels like Missing You, Sorta . . . 118
Shaky the Clown. 68	
Nostalgia 75	Blue. 120
A Whole Lot of Estrogen 77	dead dogs. 126
	Fuse. 127
The Gorilla Enclosure . . 79	Awful. 129
The trees are laughing, and the birds are telling other birds that I have no business being outside . . 84	Honey Bun 131
	Checkup #4 144
Feline. 85	
Checkup #3 90	
Nathan Roberts. 91	
Can I Stop Now?. 99	
Phallic 101	
Almost like love but more like infatuation . . 106	
A Conversation between Two Friends. . 108	
Valentine's Day 110	
Goo 116	

WELCOME TO THE CARPET BOMB EMPORIUM

....

The carpet bomb emporium is the pressure you feel at the grocery store. Before you bag up some vegetables, you notice that there are too many people and too many eyes. The confidence saved up to get some produce dwindles; before you know it, it's been months since you bought onions.

The carpet bomb emporium is seeing the most beautiful stranger. You know that you'll probably never see them again, but the way they look now is perfect, and you hope everything works out for them.

The carpet bomb emporium is wondering if anyone has ever thought this about you.

The carpet bomb emporium is the first time you were ever punched in the stomach and all the air you fought to retrieve. It's your body, how your breath smells, the grit on your teeth, laughing in the mirror, pretending that tossing over to the other side of the bed will somehow make you more tired, and the way you look up for the first time in months, realizing what season it is and how much time has passed since you've last done this and what has occurred in that time. Feeling as though you've run into an old friend, only it's slightly less comforting.

TODAY I'M SICK

. . . .

Today I'm sick. I'm sick in my body, I'm sick in the throat, I'm sick in my mouth, and I'm sick in my nose.

It's Tuesday.

I blow my sick nose into some one-ply toilet paper that's too scratchy for my tender nostrils and open up the paper to look at the thick, black sludge layering the surface of my fingers. The bathroom's yellow light bounces off the texture, and I see my reflection, and I'm black now.

"I am sludge."

The thought of morphing into a mound of sludge causes me too much stress, and I toss the paper into the toilet because I'm through with it, but it's not through with me. The gob attempts to crawl back out by slithering up the side of the rim, and I'm forced to flush, waving goodbye to my internal enemy and wishing him the best on his journey back to hell.

A scratchy pain in the farthest reaches of my throat creeps toward the light, and I cough light-green phlegm onto the sleeve of my hoodie. The sleeve has a pressed solar system of dried coughs from the morning all the way up until this moment. The new glob takes the form of me at a job I don't ever remember working, but I trust the cosmos and accept this as history. I'm wearing a name tag and a short-sleeved button-up. I hate short-sleeved button-ups. Whoever invented short-sleeved button-ups should be put into a gladiator arena with seven tigers, and the arena should be the size of my bathroom. The tigers should already be mad and have no other expression beyond anger to exhibit.

The phlegm is hardened now, and I consider what other secrets my bodily fluids might be keeping from me.

I open my mouth to see how my tongue is doing. At this point, the whole thing is light pink. I attempt to stick it closer to my nose because I'm curious what the bacteria might smell like. But I can't make anything out through my clogged nostrils. I let the tongue fall with its soggy weight, getting gray saliva all over my chin. Once I close up the shop that is my mouth, I hear a tapping that echoes from the entrance of my hole, as if somebody was knocking on my front door, and for a moment, I think this might be my first schizophrenic episode. I open wide to investigate the disturbance, and I'm relieved that the noise is just a tiny anorexic woman.

She comes crawling out, ducking under the top row of my teeth, using her hand to stabilize herself on my fangs. She's smoking a cigarette between her crooked fingers and wearing a brown shirt with black shorts, and both contain tiny rips and stains from God knows what. Her shoulders point out from under the shirt, giving her a wire-hanger frame. Her bruises smear against her leathery, gray skin like a cheap tattoo—a malnourished lizard person.

As she's about to puff on her cigarette, I begin to bite down on the miniature woman. Her frail bones crunch between my molars, and her rib cage and skull don't stand a chance against the force of my jaw. She is fast with her flailing limbs and scattered movements. But not fast enough. I chomp on something round, and chunky juice squirts onto my tongue. That must be the brain, and this becomes the first thing I taste all morning. I swallow the rest, continue with my sickness, and end the day with a migraine.

NOT TOO SURE ABOUT THIS GUY

....

Within the brief moments of one exotic feeling to the next, he eventually ends up eating rice cakes in the mirror for three hours.

Do you know what that does to a man?

Sport shorts and an old man's sweater.

A visual act of clashing a person's carefree attitude with a much more appealing and civilized persona.

The attire of the modern scholar.

A brief stop-by introspection.

But he doesn't stay for too long.

"The look I am giving you is disgust."

He sticks his tongue out at me.

"No, I won't choke you while I hold you down and fuck you! I am far more interested in where that might come from."

He thinks with his hands. His fingers tied to his rapid thoughts, twiddling them and tossing them into the air, waiting for the next twenty-dollar idea.

"We do everything we can to replicate nature instead of going into nature."

"A smart man would never move into the city, and an even smarter man would drive out into the wilderness and blow his head off."

I still think about this.

READ THE ROOM

....

Narrator: "The orange sky reflects onto the damp street of a quiet neighborhood, only projecting the faint echoes of distant vehicles sliding through the wet surfaces. Trees still drip from the previous shower, and it is as though the break in the dark clouds has allowed a moment of bliss. Fourth Street is where we meet our half-conscious protagonist, winding down from the day's exhaustion. Our protagonist rests on his couch, not quite sure what program he should melt his remaining attention into."

Man: "The ultimate balance of art can dip into satisfying violence while indulging in reflective introspection.

A man of education will find this balance genuine and fulfilling, supporting his need to create and destroy.

While trying to pass some time and not pass so much time that I have wasted, I decided to craft the perfect formula for what I wanted at the particular moment and the like moments that would allow me to be challenged. To have my thoughts stimulated while maybe even gaining some new ones. But all the while, I wanted something with violence. I want to see people get hit and screamed at. Someone stabbed or shot or maybe even just pushed.

I need to be stimulated intellectually and primitively because I am a man foremost and a "thinker" second.

There are no absolutes in our world, especially within art and life. Art is a reflection of life, and hence the circle goes back again. We are part of that circle. As Hegel states, "We learn from history that we do not learn from history." We should acknowledge as humans the internal spectrum for our capacity of love and hate, for these are equal parts of ourselves. Or we are doomed to stick within this psychotic cycle of confusion toward our actions: philosophy and violence or love and hate."

Narrator: "Once the man finished his speech and selected his desired program, he continued to devour the flesh of the homeless man's face, and it was very tasty."

GREAT IDEAS

....

A Latino gentleman told me recently that if you don't have citizenship and someone shoots at you, through the legal process, you will get paperwork that supports citizenship. I confirmed this without any testimony whatsoever and told him it was a brilliant idea. The señor arranged to meet his friend at a gas station to test his bulletproof hypothesis. They haven't done it yet, but I'm eager to hear the results.

As a child, I would hear in the media and through friends that if you have a loose tooth, your best option would be to tie a string around it. You can then link that string to a doorknob, quickly relieving the pain and suffering of having a loose tooth.

The mature side of the spectrum would be suicide. Having a firearm taped to a doorknob can quickly relieve you from the pain and suffering attached to an overstimulated and joyless life. But like a loose tooth, I found it better to let it fester annoyingly in the background until it eventually falls out.

I bought a four-dollar box of raspberries. It wasn't many raspberries for the price, certainly less than four dollars' worth. That is until I tasted them. The first one I tried gave me this intense head rush; I almost collapsed on the kitchen floor. The starving urge prevented me from taking the time to clean them properly, or myself for that matter, for I was sweaty and had a thin coat of musk sealed over my skin. This was when all my stored knowledge of the day came to a beautiful plateau. I took the berries into the shower with me, covered myself and the berries with soap, and ate the berries as I scrubbed. I eventually couldn't withstand the flavor and collapsed to the floor, which had already become a part of my routine earlier that month. Other than bruising my elbow, this did not bother me. Those soapy berries resurrected my evening. With those berries and I pressed under the warm comfort of my shower head, I was convinced that I was a genius.

SLUG

. . . .

"I caught a slime"
Holds up slug
"It's a slug"
The whole crowd laughs

GOING SHOPPING

....

I needed new clothes. Or milk. Or maybe it was peanut butter? Maybe all three.

This is what happens when I don't bother with a list. I figure once I get to the store and stand in front of some items, it will come rushing back, but I'm the same person now as I was when I initially thought this, and my brain power has not improved.

I stare into the orgy of ice-cubed dinners next to the frozen forty-year-old man. He has burritos wedged in all parts of him—Ass, love handles, thighs, and, of course, his mouth.

This is the burrito section. Even I know that.

I grab one and throw it into my basket; I assume it is man flavored.

There are too many people here, bumping around and filling up on bread, observing me as I attempt to take something off the shelf just to put it back.

How dare there be people in the same place as me? They knew I'd be getting groceries at this exact moment, and they all showed up just to foil me. Don't they know I have popcorn to buy?

I throw a few items in my basket that would impress people or make me look more attractive: protein powder, big knives, potatoes, and things of that nature. I maneuver around the store, glued to the walls. There are boyfriends with their girlfriends and husbands with their wives and pretty people dressed scantily, while the remainder is old bags of MSG and obese satiation—too much time in the burrito aisle, I think.

The exit has disappeared, so I'm forced to go to the other side of the store. It does this sometimes. The entrance occupies some relative space in time and disappears every few hours or so. I'm not sure where it goes. Neither do the employees; I've already asked them.

Nobody notices the groceries in my basket, leaving me to wonder if I should've gotten what I actually wanted. But there's no time now: soon the rest of the store will disappear in on itself. The whole store occupies a similar space to the entrance but is just perceived at different times. I know it's sort of an inconvenience to have a store recede into the cosmos annually, but you just can't beat those prices.

While moving through the aisles and avoiding eye contact with the shoppers, I can already see the transformation from regular grocery architecture into the peanut butter aisle. The walls at the entrance turn to a tan concrete, while the texture smooths out until eventually becoming towering globs of creamy goop. The top shelves are melted from the lights, oozing down on the different brands and onto the cadavers of those who got caught up in the metamorphosis.

Poor shoppers who now live on as the chunky contents of various peanut butter brands.

The smell is a terrorist attack on my senses, and I figure I can only spend so much time here before I, too, become an amorphous mound of sweet and creamy. Each step sinks into the floor more than the last, but my determination for what I might need keeps me moving.

I desire carbohydrates, dunk my pinkie finger into the floor and suck off the encapsulating coating. It's not too bad, and this is enough to boost my energy. Once I reach the back of the aisle, I turn to ensure the store still resides on this plane. All I can make out is the warm gobs dripping onto the other mounds of cream. I fear my shopping is coming to an end.

At this moment, I begin to sink into the floor.

I've stood in one place for too long. I should've paid attention to the sign on the wall. The sign had a picture of a man sinking into the floor. The caption read, "Don't stand in one place for too long." While I slowly sink into the tan abyss, I stretch out my limbs and grasp a container of chunky butter. I think it's my favorite brand.

The slippery goo rises under my hip bone, and the momentum from my lower body pulls me down even faster. I quickly rip open the packaging and plunge my pointer finger downward, fishing out a large glob. It indeed does look like chunky butter.

Now I'm nearly engulfed in the abyss. Soon I will be like the other foolish men who went looking for glory and condiments. But before it can have me, I shove the butter into my mouth and swish it around, tasting the sweet glory.

I had it before it had me. I have consumed the abyss.

COMING TO TERMS

....

Two men in their late twenties sit outside of a coffee shop. It's early October; the sun shines promisingly through a cluster of damp clouds hanging over them. A few dried leaves lie wedged between the legs of their chairs. It's mostly quiet and peaceful as the men sip their coffee and keep to themselves.

Man 1: *sighs*

Man 2: Cut that shit out.

Man 1: Where?

Man 2: What? No, I mean you! Cut that shit out!

Man 1: How about you lay off? All I'm doing is breathing, and you find some way to turn that into a problem!

Man 2: What do you need to be sighing about? Is your life so Goddamn hard that you have to moan about every little thing? Are you being tortured? Is your family being held captive by terrorists? Do you have some biohazardous new form of testicular cancer?

Man 1: You're psychotic! It's not a weakness or some sort of bitch and moan. I'm sighing! I'm fucking tired, and people can be fucking tired. You're so full of your own shit; it's spraying out your ears! If you say you never get tired or feel the urge to exhale air out of your nose, then you're a bigger prick than that guy over there.

Man 1: *points at the older gentleman sitting at the table across from them*

Man 3: If I may interject. I believe both of you are completely in the wrong.

The man pulls a chair from his table. He's a tall, skinny, white-haired Caucasian, and he's got on a heavy, dark-green rain jacket and some light-blue jeans splattered with just a little bit of white paint.

Man 3: Now, how can both of you gentlemen sit here and argue about such foolishness? How does something so small as a release of air bother you? Does it really affect you in any remarkable way? And you, acting as if your life is so terribly exhausting. You're out here on a beautiful fall day, absorbing the air into your lungs, and all you can do is reflect on what's stressing you out. Heaven forbid we have the smallest amount of discomfort in our lives. May God help both of you; you two really think your voices are so important to where you feel the need to impose your morphed values onto each other. How about you try to take in this afternoon's sublime love and reflect that onto each other instead of sitting and letting your demons get the best of you? Now, I must go and get as far away from you, gentlemen, as I possibly can before I, too, turn into an entitled faggot.

MEETING

....

The fidgeting plethora of zipping zippers and the mumbled chatter of previous arbitrary complaints fill the white noise. The older gentleman next to me began to overshare how much money he was making at my age. I give him a pseudo-courtesy smile. The type that says "fuck off" more than it says "please, tell me more."

The man has little white crusty skin flakes blanketing his shoulders. I try my hardest not to seem interested, but his enjoyment from sucking up my air skews his awareness.

After a few moments drag on, our boss eventually takes his magnificent malnourished body to the front of the room. He wobbles and snarls like a goblin from Middle-earth. I want so badly to unsheathe my steel and split his melon in two, all along the spreadsheets and laptop chargers.

Only then will I be knighted by the account manager and destined to protect my office corridors from evil spirits and cursed demons.

Once I am knighted, I will smite down the cults of canceling forked tongues and restore this facility to its once-holy origins.

But for now, I should probably attempt to pay attention.

THE SICK SIR

· · · · · · · · · · · · · · · · · · · ·

The Seattle area is the resting ground for a slew of homeless Seattleites, varying in all breeds, from the ones who say "God bless ya" and tell you to have a nice day to the ones that chase you down the street, yelling about all the different ways they'll fuck your mother. My experience is with the latter. But this drifter, in particular, deserves a category of his own. This man had more bravado than any ordinary bum: a curated persona of erratic insight with a unique complexity behind the eyes. A complexity that far exceeds flat-out opioid psychosis.

It was a few Friday nights ago when our paths crossed. I was spending time with some "friends," and we were enduring each other's company with some help from our routine drinks and pseudo-political debates, which usually went nowhere. Immediately after standing to make my great escape, my senses were assaulted by the night's limitations.

My inebriation closed in on my blurry world; I only wanted to get home and scarf down something greasy. About ten minutes had passed since we had all separated when I began to notice the lack of barhoppers around me. Without the sprawling groups of obnoxious twenty-somethings, I was free to take up as much space on the sidewalk as humanly possible.

This would have been more entertaining if it hadn't been so quiet. No slurred chatter to fall into the background and no breadcrumbs of open stores illuminating my journey back home. Besides the lingering stench of spilled trash, my lone stumbling steps were my only company.

I continued, and the more I descended the street, the more I could distinguish a faint voice. With my contingent vision, I locked onto a dim streetlight outlining a lone straggler. Maybe a confused and lost drunk.

I suddenly felt kindred to the dark outline. We were two of the same: brothers of the night. I laughed, telling myself I was hilarious and continued down the street. Within proximity, the speech's cadence shifted. It had gone from unrecognizable ranting to a stern and disciplined lecturing you'd expect to get after pissing off a teacher or a stepparent. Although I was no longer alone, I was starting to wish I was.

I reduced my steps as the feeling of fight or flight revealed my instinctual cowardice, and I halted under the flickering light, not five feet between the stranger and me. He continued waving his mug and spitting into the black street, and I was trespassing here. The man towered over me with his paper-thin physique, and I knowingly questioned my masculinity. He was dressed in an old brown suit laced with thin pinstripes, broken and faded by city filth.

His cheekbones protruded from his face with sharp, almost right angles and perfect symmetry. Part of me was a little jealous. He clutched a large black Bible in one hand and an empty coffee mug in the other. Printed on it was big cheap text: "Don't talk to me till I had my coffee."

Nobody's talking to you.

I chuckle at the irony. I can't help but watch while he indulges in some strange performance art, shouting about "God's will" and the "temptations of Lucifer." At least those were the keywords I could make out. The mix of his grating voice and old English was difficult to discern, but he spoke with so much fervor that even I was starting to question my choices. Judging by his performance and direction of energy, I wasn't his target demographic. He was mainly faced away from me, unaware of my presence. It was almost as if his projections had cast a live studio audience along the street, and he was tonight's host. I chuckled again.

This time he noticed me, and he locked his eyes with mine. Without breaking eye contact, the priest glided over to me with his big, long, skeleton legs, and in two giant steps, he planted himself, only inches from my face, wrapped into his dead, decaying cloud of musk.

I was still holding his gaze. He gripped my shoulder, fitting his thumb snugly into the pocket of my collar. He fucking stank, and I could see the dried-up skin accumulating around the creases of his nose and mouth. I was half expecting a little termite to come crawling out from the patches of hair where a beard would typically be. He dug his paws deep into my shoulder and leaned into where I could see the discoloration of his clogged pores and my reflection in his pupils. I looked like a scared bitch. Then he whispered,

"The sick sir lust for the desolation of all saints and where thee resign

Thy children feareth ill, sir, for that gent is the one blanketed in darkness, pondering the engulfment of the pureness in thine joyful souls

Ye sick sir only observes the black of the human raceth, ye col'r yond hides und'r the heaviest stone

That gent burdens thy stone upon broad shouldst'rs

F'r at which hour that gent rest

that gent is did crush

eareth the sick sir and alloweth le thee beest a warning to whomever may crosseth thy path

For that gent bares a familiar grineth

Less yond grineth is of the unholy damn'd."

We basked in silence for a moment, letting his hot breath stick to the surface of my skin, waiting for something else to happen. I thought it was my turn to speak, so I said the first thing that came to mind.

"Will you take a gift card?"

CHECKUP #1

....

Hello. Welcome to your first checkup. I hope I am finding you at a pleasant moment in whatever thoughts the day has led you to. What exactly are those thoughts? How has the week been for you? And how would you describe your current state of being?

Take your time.

If you have trouble, then we can revisit.

Overthinking these questions is impossible.

How the room smells.

The oil on your forehead.

The way the pages or screen feels on the tips of your fingers.

And yes, I'm well aware that you are reading a narrative.

But worry not about what my voice means in the narrative context.

For I am simply a voice with the purpose of attempting to check up on you.

I hope you are well.

Until next time.

CHURCH GIRL

....

I spent the morning giving praise to my savior. I wept uncontrollably while we sang songs in his name, and I don't think I've ever felt this close to my family at church. We donated our loose bills and time to aid the service and did anything else we could have done to help.

We all grew closer today.

Not only with God himself but with one another as well.

Now get over here and fuck my whore ass.

WE LIVE IN A MATERIAL WORLD, AND I'M A MECHANICAL GORILLA TEARING OUT HER INNER WORKINGS TO GET REVENGE ON HER CREATOR.

....

You have perfectly shaped arms; I bet they're good for ripping and tearing.

There's a sound about the equivalent of a rusted scalpel dragging onto sheet metal.

I would be delighted if, one day, you came with me to get grocery bags of copper wire and steel wool. We will share a bottle of wine as I sauté the copper with garlic and butter. The tiny kitchen will get too hot, and you'll become hungry as soon as the butter and garlic hit the pan.

An ancient absurdity consumes a single mother when she rests with her rubber child at the park.

A group of crows is called a murder, and that's also what I call the thing I did to a homeless man last week.

I sometimes imagine a mad scientist who's very good at creating experiments, but he struggles with the practical aspects of connecting hypotheses to his variables, never really following through to the end. I imagine this because I'm not good at science, so imagining something slightly out of the realm of possibility gives me confidence. When I'm lonely, I imagine that he builds the perfect bride. She's perfect because she supports and trusts him, as he does for her. Sometimes they make eye contact unexpectedly, and neither can help but smile. His work improves because of this, although there is an unsubstantial trade-off. She's a giant mechanical gorilla who has brief moments of intense rage. She throws tables and destroys his hard, unfinished work. One night her rage is so out of control that the scientist begins to fear for his own life. In one final attempt to help her and free her of this animal's temper, he decides to discipline himself and create an experiment that will fix her internal hard wiring. He works all night, sweat covers his sheets of failed theories, but he knows he's getting closer. When the giant mechanical wife finds him working, she assumes he's trying to destroy her. In a breach of rage, she begins tearing out her internal hardware, throwing metal across the room, and crying tears of oil and betrayal. Before the scientist's loving eyes, the gorilla wife turns herself into a hunk of scrap metal on the laboratory floor—a heartbreaking clutter of discarded materials and another failed experiment splayed at the scientist's feet.

I think about this quite often.

ANIMAL

. . . .

Girl: Yeah, I was watching a commercial the other day, and I saw that one guy from the Muppets. You know, with the crazy hair.

Boy: Ok.

Girl: What's his name?

Boy: With the crazy hair?

Girl: Yeah.

Boy: The animal.

Girl: The animal? Are you sure?

Boy: Yeah.

Girl: That's kinda boring.

Boy: No.

Girl: Cause he's like a crazy animal?

Boy: No, it's because he murdered thirteen children in the 1970s.

LOGIC

....

Are you overweight and unsatisfied with your body? Does your torso spill out over the side of your waistband?

Does the thought of getting up an hour early to go on a run fill you with dread?

Then you might as well set flame to your body. Make sure you either call 911 ahead of time or go to a public area where people can call for help. Then when you're in the hospital, and the doctors are performing a skin graft, they'll need to pull the skin from all different areas. Then you should be able to look a little bit thinner or at least shed a few pounds unless you'd rather choose a bland diet or go on a treadmill. Yuck!

So what are you waiting for? Go set that disgusting body up in flames!

CIRCUS

....

One of the clowns sits on a red stool, eating a peanut butter and jelly sandwich that his clown wife made him.

A large lion tears through the crowd as peanuts and limbs fly through circular hoops.

I spill a large bag of warm kettle corn onto a mother breastfeeding her child.

An impish man is made fun of by teenagers.

Some heavyset male finishes a half-eaten elephant ear resting naked on a table, still glazed to perfection.

All in all, I had a great time on the field trip.

THE DAY I FROZE TIME

If I remember right, it was on a Thursday afternoon. It happened during the period of pre-weekend warmth, the same fervor that filled the highways with traffic and the grocery stores with workers buying six-packs in celebration of another week shoved back into memory.

The switch appeared in front of me, and like any other curious being would do, I flipped it, and time ceased to continue. I wandered the parks, poked people in the back, took lollipops out of children's hands and skipped down the street to pet all the dogs I could find. I even let myself flirt with an attractive, younger woman who otherwise wouldn't have allowed me.

With so much time on my hands, I decided to use it properly and allowed myself to be exactly where I was for as long as I needed—something that no other person but me was able to experience. To wait in one particular moment. To think about where I was standing, not to be perceived by anyone. Almost as if I took up no space at all. Eventually, I got bored. Despite the endless possibilities presented, I struggled with allowing myself to indulge in the entertainment. I moved back to the switch, and I flipped it. Therefore time continued to move, and the switch disappeared.

Everything seems to move so fast now, and I still struggle to slow down as I was able to before. I miss the prolonged relishing of a simple afternoon and the comforting isolation of an infinite moment. That was two years ago, and I haven't seen the switch since, and I regret ever flipping the switch to normalcy. I hope someday I'll be able to see that switch again and enjoy another moment of stillness.

THE BIRD DREAM

....

Dominic Shultz sits his old tired ass on his old tired couch. The light of the outside world maintains his home as a warm sanctuary for his slothfulness. He vanishes into a special on the nature channel about the conflict between species of birds. Enthralled by the brand-new world of creatures he had previously overlooked, Dominic's attention jumps from fact to fact, allowing the train of intellectual stimulation to plow through every stop, reveling in the impression of enlightenment, thriving in the idiocy of unprofitable wisdom.

Dominic watches a mother pigeon on the program caring for her babies. She keeps them warm under her weight and stays alert for any potential danger. Once all the babies are tucked in and their marbled eyes close to a soft line of infantile peace, she leaps from the nest and ventures out into the wilderness to fetch dinner. The young patiently huddle together against the night and form one large bunch of innocent fur, anticipating the delivery of their vomitus delight. Dominic doesn't blink or glance away from the screen, losing himself in what it might be like to live as one of those baby birds. He imagines his head on a baby bird's torso, flapping his little bird wings and cuddling with his siblings. To be safe inside all day. To have all your meals brought to you by your loving mother. To be loved and protected. That is the bird's dream.

Dominic's daydream defrosts over his window of reality through the program's severe shift in tone. The royalty-free soundtrack contorts into a webbing of malevolent strings as the hidden "Nature Cam," now a nightmare cam, transforms the environment into a green Wachowski-esque hell. Dominic's senses are under attack, and his previous confidence in the birds' safety weakens like the structural integrity of a former crack house.

He scans the tree line for danger, starting from the left side of the screen, maintaining a vigilant eye for any movement. There doesn't seem to be any immediate threat beyond the still eeriness of the forest. His eyes reach the center of the screen, where a woodpecker arises from the infernal regions.

The demon breaches the confines of the nest with eyes full of carnage and holocaust. Dominic fixates on the children, rubbing his sweaty palms onto his pajama bottoms, knowing that nothing can be done to prevent nature from completing her cycle. Once the beast establishes its prey and sows the seeds of torture, nothing is left but to plunge into the furry innocence. The woodpecker sets forth its speared beak into the defenseless babies, jackhammering its way through the pile, tearing the feathers into the air, and spewing specks of pubescent blood across their home. The little siblings don't have the strength to defend themselves and try to run, but there is no escape from the rapid thrust of the woodpecker's bill. They can only chirp for their mother to return and save them from this nefarious fate.

The screams bounce off the walls of his home and echo throughout his heart. Those terrified screams and they'll never leave his memory.

No justice in the world could make up for this gruesome act of barbarism. They are just babies and innocent babies waiting for some vomit. Dominic shoots up from the couch, pulling a muscle in the process.

"Leave them alone!"

His objection results in spit hitting the television as the violence ensues through the moisture.

He grabs the remote and presses the power button with so much force that it jams into the plastic.

Dominic has had more than enough TV for one day.

CANCER SCARE

....

Best-case scenario, I die.

MY PINK EYE

....

In a visual medium, whenever a character is waking up from a slumber, and the audience can view the space they reside in, there's usually a semblance of an eye-opening. As if ordinary people greet the morning with slow, methodical eyelid raises. Imagine that for the sake of drama and world-building, but now only half the space is being occupied. Maybe the character had only one eye or something obstructing that part of their vision, right? I'm not too keen on the practical aspects of visual storytelling. But imagine it nonetheless.

It was a blur, as it usually is. The stark shock of entering another day and the confusion accompanying your brain slowly powering on. Sort of a pseudo-birth. I stumbled to the bathroom as the light from the street pathetically illuminated my heavy, repressed stream of burning urine. Something was off, and that something had just so effortlessly breached its way into my morning, storming the trenches of routine and destroying my defensive lines. But what was it? It wasn't that I had fallen asleep in clothes and then woke with nothing on; it wasn't the new mole that had sprouted on my upper thigh. It was something else. Whether I followed it or not, my schedule was meticulous, and it would be pretty apparent if there were something unaccomplished or out of place, as there usually was.

I slapped on the bathroom light and was welcomed to the dismay of my reflection. My pitiful, puffy self, except my left eye, was swollen from top to bottom, and, looking at it with more intent, I could conclude the origins of my obstructed sight. Feelings of agitation took hostage of my senses, similar to when somebody noticed their blood bag at the donation center. It's impressive the amount of pain we could hide when we were not completely aware of our situation. A headache came screaming from the back of my brain, resembling that of a caffeine addict's peak withdrawals, almost as if a tiny homunculus Zeus was summoning his prolific strength. The ocean tides thumping against my temples.

Despite the pain I was in and the sound of the currents in my ears, I chose to divert my attention to the obstruction: an enormous red oval where my eye used to be and the small black line that separated it horizontally. It was as if my eye was being sucked into a forbidden region beyond Earth's solar system.

I dug my fingers inward to separate the lids, but first, I had to pick away cemented green gunk from all the night's buildup. I didn't even bother washing my hands. Despite having visible dirt under my nails, I scraped away. God, it hurts. I eventually tore away at the mucus rocks, and I could see some white, or what was left of it. Red, jagged strings of lightning suffering now possessed the surface of the gooey white of my eye. My sight peeked through the foggy, cracked lens, and I placed my fingers higher on my lids and began to pull them apart. The eye, being separated, revealed webs of fresh pus, and I cried yellow tears of bacterial ooze. With each new stream came unbearable pain and embarrassment. This should not happen to average humans. This should occur only to homeless bums sleeping in alleyways with pillows of piss-soaked cardboard, not some customer service rep who took too long to wash his pillowcase. I felt like there might be a joke there. But before I could think of one, a web of stringy gunk shot onto the mirror like the decades of buildup from grandpa's sebaceous cyst. At this moment, I was Spider-Man's handicapped cousin.

There was nothing like some good self-surgery to remind yourself just how disgusting you really are. My favorite example growing up was giving myself ingrown toenails and performing the operation myself. The process began by picking at the desired nail, letting all the gnarled bits fill in the crevice by the skin, and waiting about a week or two until the red swelling plateaued. The twinkle in my eye I procured from feeling the burning pain in my shoes was like that of getting to pick what movie to watch on family night. My tools consisted of miscellaneous objects from my escapades. My mom's sewing needle, plastic safety scissors, and my younger sister's eyebrow tweezers. Of course, they were never washed. My primary method of operation consisted of scraping away at the fat that ruptured under the damned nail with the relentlessly sharp needle, then sticking in the tweezers to help pull the fat ajar from the toenail. Now that I had some more room to work with, I was able to finish. I'd stick the scissors into the side of the nail that met with the skin and lift it. With the tweezers, I could pull out anything that looked askew and scrape the nail back to perfection. Through all my experience and education, I had become something of a professional and never had to visit the doc's office once.

I eventually let the lids recede over my pupil and hinder my vision once again. It looked like I'd be calling out of work today, but at least there was a valid reason. No sick voice or heart-beating anticipation of the eventual call. They could always tell the phoniness in your voice. Stumbling to the phone, I called my supervisor to let him hear the good news. After some ringing, he finally picked up his signature nasally and annoyed tone.

"Supervisor Paul speaking."

"Hey, Paul, it's Mike."

My name is Mike, by the way.

There was a short pause like he was mustering up composure, biting his tongue to repress his inner hell.

"Hey."

"Hi, I'm just calling in to let you know that I'm sick."

"Ok"

If he wasn't annoyed before, he was now. I could tell by his huff of diabetic breath.

"Yeah, sorry."

I gestured insincerely.

"Do you have PTO and a doctor's note?"

"I have PTO and pink eye."

"Do you have a doctor's note?'

"Do I need one?"

"In order to call out, you need a doctor's note, or else it's a write-up."

Worthless prick.

"I don't think you understand. My eye is pink, and I don't need a doctor to look at my eye and tell me the same thing."

"I need a note inorder not to write you up, and by looking at your account, you are one write-up away from termination."

I knew he was smiling his fat, fucking face right after that.

"Can I just send you a picture?"

"No, thank you, I don't want to see that."

"Ok, Paul, man to man, I'm not coming in with this nasty infection, and I'm not going to the doctor's and paying $350 to have someone tell me what's already obvious. Now. If you don't want me to go down there to spray yellow slime on everything I come into contact with, then

I suggest you kindly put me down in the system as sick. Or, instead, I can go down there and make you the first victim of my bacterial revenge. You don't want that, do you, Paul?"

It was silent on the other line except for his heavy, wet breath and my depleting fire, making me lose confidence in my objection. That was until he began to speak.

"I understand."

"Thank you."

"And I do apologize for how you're feeling. Please get well soon. For the company. Because we all need you."

"Um, wow, ok. Thank you, I couldn't have said it better myself."

His tone dropped into a bare and stark manner. My pores flushed, and my arms developed goose bumps. Like somebody else had taken control of his spineless persona.

"Now, what are we gonna do about this eye?"

POINT OF VIEW FROM A CANNIBAL

....

Things have been going pretty well lately, and I don't have much outside of the average tedium to complain about. As of now, I'm in one of those plain boring states where not much is happening.

I totally devoured this seven-year-old blond boy earlier this week. I took him right off the swing set on the playground downtown. Can you believe that? No supervision or anything. He practically swung right into my mouth.

He tasted fine.

I saw the cute young lady that works at register eight today—the one with the red hair and cute, little, splattered freckles.

She raised her eyebrows at me, and I did it back. Some people may see that as a regular human interaction, but not for us. I think we have our own unique language through small facial movements and subtle glances.

For example.

Eyebrows angled down in a scowl: she's sad and wants me to ask her what's wrong.

Nose twitch left: she's having a good day.

Nose twitch right: she's having a bad day.

One eyebrow up: she had been thinking about me all week.

Both eyebrows raised: she's in love, and she's been waiting for me.

She's so sweet.

I wonder if she'll let me eat her.

NECRO

....

I'm dead.

I'm a withering corpse, rotting away from the bone. Quite literally. I'm a decaying young man. Please don't ask me about the technicalities of my thoughts. Everyone does, and it's far too tiresome. Just let me talk aloud to the abyss in front of and within me.

I was still relatively young when I was tossed down here by the living. In my second year of college, I majored in business marketing. I definitely could have had sex a few more times before biting it. But who doesn't have a few regrets? The lack of vaginal action isn't what bothers me. It's that those bastards get to walk in the sun without the slightest idea of when they might end up like me—living in constant uncertainty no definitive answers within the cosmic aperture of unpredictability. I suppose some intellectual might tell you that's what makes it so beautiful. While that's very true at the moment, you eventually end up in my position, and all the questions, predictions, religions, and ghost stories turn to fairy dust. There are only answers down here—claustrophobic oblivion.

But on the bright side, I got an open casket. Some poor bastards aren't given the satisfaction of having their loved ones cry over their tailored suits and movie star makeup. It makes me feel bad for all those other guys and gals. The ones who had their skulls caved in by some psycho, or those who were distracted driving and flew through the windshield, face surfing against the concrete like a big red piece of chalk.

Not strictly anybody's ideal entry into the afterlife.

If I knew I was going to bite it and got to choose the perfect scenario, I would have to set some sort of record, so not only would I pop up in the obituaries but also on some website or some book, topping some other idiot. Something like the most backflips achieved on a suicide jump or most sleeping pills taken before the flatline. They would pump my stomach, sounding like one of those coin machines at a grocery store. Or a gravel truck dumping its last shipment at the job site.

Not much I can do about it now, however. *Now* doesn't mean much of anything anymore. I wait for my coffin to cave in on me, and my body eventually becomes the melting pot for hundreds of insects.

If I'm being sincere, it's nice to know that I'll be a home for these little critters and all their offspring.

All my dreams for nature to reclaim
Sucking into the gray flesh
Warm moisture cradling them to sleep
The wicked smooth bone picked clean
the fleeting stench of youth
My own private Los Angeles.

OPEN-HEART SURGERY FOR THE CALORIC GLUTTON

....

I'm dying. Well, maybe. Most likely. I've been blessed with shambled and uneven heartbeats, also known as arrhythmia. My heart marches to the beat of its own drum, and the electrical currents that are supposed to regulate an average rhythm just decide not to work, often leaving my body in total disarray. The best way I can describe it is that it's very rare that I ride that line of heart rate normality. Instead, I go from what feels like a hoof on a horse track to being void of feeling altogether.

This might sound frustrating and painful, and although I adore the sympathy and attention from others, I try to keep the self-pity to a minimum, considering that I wouldn't be in this situation if I had only done a better job at maintaining proper jurisdiction of my health. This thing I refer to as my body has become the receptacle for phthalates and hydrolyzed proteins, the results of my bad habits put into effect by socially acceptable poison, all within arm's reach. My lifestyle is primarily sedentary and unmotivated. I can't remember the last time I got down and did some push-ups or stretched out my beautiful cankles. I don't own a pair of running shoes or any sports equipment, although I do have a Little League baseball bat, and there was one time when I bought one of those hand-gripper things, the ones you squeeze while sitting at your desk. It's like a forearm workout, I guess. I bought that with the expectation of getting super-veiny muscle-guy arms. Those arms that seem to be more attractive to men than they do to women. I used it for only a couple of weeks before I lost it. At least I tried. I don't do much of that anymore.

Then I had my breakthrough. After years of punishing my body like the caloric whore it is, I eventually concluded that the fate of my body was sealed, and there was nothing to be done. An unavoidable anomaly brought on by sheer chance, unbeknownst to myself and my always sweaty chest. That's sarcasm. And I am fully aware of the gluttonous globe I have now become. I'm picking up an easy form of coping with my sickness in the shape of comedic relief. It's a work in progress, but I think by the time I bite it, I should be this generation's Curly Howard, which should be very soon.

In approximately ten minutes, my chest will be pried open by clinical meat hooks while I lie in a deep sleep, letting the doctors gladly poke around inside of me and squirt my blood over each other as they allow the nurses to shake their bloody chests in my unconscious face. If only. That was in a dream I had, and a perfect one at that.

The dream ended in me being perfectly fine after the procedure and going to live a super happy and healthy life, even developing a six-pack in the process. This allowed me to pick up girls from bars and not call them after we slept together. Not because I'm a prick but because we mutually understood how deep our connection was and where our boundaries lay.

Just like what the great philosophers spoke of.

The simple truth was that there was a slim-to-none chance that this procedure would work. Under my condition, it was possible that I would drop dead, and the doctors would have to grind me up into little McDonald's burgers right there.

Now I'm hungry, and this is the problem.

"Good morning."

A chipper voice erupts into the waiting room, momentarily breaking the trance between the patrons and their screens. When I look up, I'm greeted by a man in doctor cosplay approaching me with his hand all the way extended, despite still being several feet away. Nobody should ever be this happy.

"Hi," I spurted to him, already knowing everything about him by the way he bared his teeth.

"If you'll follow me, we're now ready for you."

As I stand up, the doctor grips my hand and takes me down the hallway as if he's afraid I'll wander off.

"You don't need to hold my hand."

"It's quite all right," he assures me, interlocking his fingers with mine and squeezing. Not the painful type of squeeze but the secure type, so if I did consider wandering off, he could guide me back to the correct path.

This is the closest I've been to another person in a very long time. My hands begin to sweat. All the excitement starts to make my heart beat erratically, and I get nervous that I'll die before we can begin the procedure. What difference does it make?

The doctor guides me into a room where I assume I will spend the next several hours. Upon my entry, I'm greeted by three nurses with friendly smiles, putting on gloves and adjusting the nearby equipment. One of them is very attractive, and I take a moment to imagine she's shaking her chest in my face while I lay unconscious. I think I stare for too long because they start to look at me, then back at each other. The doctor lets go of my hand, and now I feel naked.

"Put this on; then you can lie down right here for a moment, and we'll get everything ready for you."

I say nothing and go lie down where I'm told, letting the professionals gather their gadgets and collect their materials while doubt and shame creep their way into the back of my mind and my back fat. I know I will die. Because, of course, Murphy's law is the only divine truth. This is what I deserve for treating life so trivially. No passion, no effort. Just feeling terrible about myself, stressed, sweating into the mattress, and getting up only to eat and shit. A curdled mass absorbing all trans fats within a five-mile radius or however far the delivery can reach. But I'd be lying to myself if I said I didn't sorta love it. No worries at all, constantly shoveling sweets into my face. Yeah. That's not so bad. I lived to the fullest. I did what I wanted, and that's more than most people can say about their lives. Mom would be proud—more sarcasm.

"I'm ready, Doc!" I shout across the room, the nurses looking confused again. I decided to milk this moment of confidence, for I don't know how long it'll last.

"Stick it in me; I'm ready to go under."

"Well, someone's eager, aren't they? I'm just about ready."

With a large needle and a big Disneyland grin, he struts my way, almost skipping, and I imagine he trips and crams the needle into his jugular. He straddles the chair next to me, reverse cowgirl style.

"Now, this will put you under for the next several hours. You'll be out like a light until we have one hundred percent completed the procedure and then some."

"Don't you guys normally use gas or something? You know, like, whatever the hell is inside of balloons." I imagine balloons at the fair, and then I imagine fair food. Now I'm hungry again, and this is the problem.

"Well, we used to, but we recently adopted this new serum. It's carefully designed to put the subject under without any discrepancies. No need to worry. I recommend this over the old silly gas any day, and I'm a doctor."

He laughs a little too hard, and I swear I can smell the coffee through his mask.

"Hey, if you say so."

I look down, and he's already plunged the stinger into me, and I pretend I'm taking a massive hit of heroin. I even bite my lip and moan. But before I can finish ignoring the pain, my eyelids slam shut, and the world around me is gone.

And back again. I wake up in an empty room. It's cold; the only sound is the beeping from a large machine. I should be dead, and the space should be a black, endless infinity, but it's all still here. I suppose the breakthrough in modern medicine has fallen short of my expectations. I'm a little disappointed; life never really goes how you expect, but come on. I was right there. So close. Ready to greet death with open arms. Yet here I am. In this unbearably cold room. Why the fuck is it so cold?

I can hardly move my limbs—or my neck, for that matter. It's like trying to piss with a hard-on; it almost hurts, and it feels like something might come out, and you're just so Goddamn hard, you're better off just waiting. To make matters even worse, I smell burgers. At least, I think it's burgers: something covered in grease. Now I'm hungry.

"Hello?"

My attempt to call out just sort of translates to a drooling moan. In another effort, I drop my bottom jaw, and rather than saying anything, a long string of saliva pours out from a puddle accumulated in the crevice of my cheeks. In my final attempt to get something done, I send my jaw into my chest and force my head up. I'm greeted with a shock that usually takes a couple of minutes to set in, but the animalistic stinging arrives early. The needles of fear stick under my fat skin. Down the center of my chest is a fleshy Grand Canyon, skin and bone pulled back to opposite sides of my torso by great shiny meat hooks. The cold instruments plunge into the numb flesh. No pain, just pressure. Sharp rods and enlarged tweezers remain trapped inside me like mechanics hard at work. The sight and my head begin to weigh too much on me, and I drop back down to the pillow.

I think for a moment that I'm having some weird fucked-up dream, and it's too much for my doped-up brain to take. It's a whole new part of myself that a living person is never supposed to see. So I must not be alive, right? But knowing my luck, this is the fresh start to a new chapter of my shit life. Thank God I'm as high as a kite.

Another chill glides through the room, this time racking around inside of me. The door is swung open, and laughter breaks into the developed tension. I maneuver my right eye to where I can vaguely see the doorframe.

The doctor walks into the room backward, almost moonwalking, facing the nurses behind him. They laugh with one another until they notice me.

The smiles leap from their faces. The doctor continues with his shtick before he looks up at me and then down at my tender chest. They all carry separate bags of McDonald's and the new seasonal milkshake I've been dying to try. No words leave my mouth. And they follow. What's there to say? There isn't a proper response in the human handbook to reclaim sanity in a situation like this. The nurses seem to get this and look to the doctor for guidance. Of course. Surely a man of this ilk should know what to do.

The doctor cracks his signature smile and exclaims, "I guess I forgot to get you something, huh, big guy?"

PIKE

. . . .

He squints his crusted eyes to the point that all the muck and grime of a night's sleep begin infringing on his poor vision.

The sun melts through the cold air and burns away the millions of wrinkles from all his nights on Pike Street.

A biker in the roadway brings a line of commuters to an almost complete stop.

The man in the car directly behind looks as though this inconvenience is God's punishment.

He snarls and hunches over the wheel as if he needs to get closer to the biker to hate him.

The sky breaks open, and the clouds part from one another.

The cold blueness reveals itself to the man.

So do the million little black blemishes soaring high.

The sight humbles the old man, and the fresh air seems so strange and foreign when compared to his dusty confines.

He stretches his jowls open to fill his Swiss-cheese lungs with coldness and brings his mouth back down with a dry stickiness.

He is smiling as he recedes into his apartment.

Falling deep asleep to the score of the city.

CHECKUP #2

....

Hello there.
It's nice to be a voice in your head again.
Or the words filling the room.
Either way.
I like it here.
What about you?
Do you enjoy having me here?
Do you need the extra company?
Or are you just perfectly fine without it?
I'm sorry.
I didn't mean to sound hostile or aggressive. Don't be upset with me.
I just want to check up and ask you some questions.
Because nobody ever does with me. If I'm telling you the truth, it's pretty awful here.
I probably shouldn't have told you any of that.
Let's just pretend that didn't happen, ok?

CONTACT HIGH

....

Thursday afternoons are usually the days I visit the park. Around this time, I'm in my most reflective and balanced state, with the weekend drawing near and the small victory of another workweek under my belt, allowing me to rationalize my positivity. These walks have become an integral part of my tight schedule of work, home, work, and home again. This dedication allows me to feel latex-tight control over my life. I get to feel like a real man who has responsibilities and duties. Duties beyond myself. Although I'm not sure what my company does, I know it's an honorable profession! People always tell me, and I also begin to believe it. Almost as if they put a vital idea within me, and now it's part of my identity. Opinions are beautiful in that way.

    I rest on a sticky bench under a large tree. The branches project a random but serene pattern onto my legs and the garbage can beside me. The lid is more or less resting on a mound of fast-food bags and disposable vape pen packages. My stomach growls. It reminds me of my lovely diet. Sometimes if I don't want to make food at home or if I don't have time, I'll stop and get some burgers and fries. An unmatched feeling of joy and accomplishment overtakes me when I bite into that soaked patty of estrogen heaven. I feel strong and replenished, and my thoughts are more transparent and rational. It reminds me of that silly sculpture of that buff guy thinking.

Around the park are cliques of city dwellers mingling with their cell phone–driven personas. This is a beautiful sight; I smile like a handsome man in a Hollywood movie. People come here to relax and escape the constraint of daily psychosis. Even out in the unmeasurable wilderness, the common folk can't escape the constant distraction of overstimulation, turning a family's ability to produce dopamine into a dollar store toy, making the delusion that technology has brought into our lives even better when shared. This is my utopia. My abundance of resources raped my views of the self, turning me into a schizophrenic fiend, and I honestly couldn't be happier.

I bring all the contaminated air into my nose and onto the back of my throat; I take the .38 Special from my jacket pocket, place the chrome barrel into my mouth, bite down on the steel architecture, and squeeze.

DUCK WADDLERS

skintight pressed thighs

a stretching heat flies through the stitching

a curdled-milk tidal wave of pimply abandon

thump thump thumping

the plastic and metal begin to rattle

the heavy breath of nachos and chowder

it's a sad sight to see

anger and depression fill up their beaks

and long hot days

spurt oil from their cheeks

the children scream and stare

for they have found

the duck waddlers

FEEL THE BURN

....

the moral holiday of tinnitus innuendo soon expires

wasted confidence that melts off the walls

into the cheap laminate of a coated Sunday

the broken thermostat sends me scurrying to my clothes pile

spider reconnaissance comes once again for my sugar wrappers

and I know summer is closing in

an arched hunch makes for a perfect Hot Wheels track

off the shoulders onto the desk where my diverted focus resides

remaining outside of ego responsibility

I walked five times this week to balance out the sweet

moods of dreary and dull

there was a feline askew along the windowsill

the sun came through and cooked it to rest

then foolishly returned to a blue night-light of a four runtime

Sweet dreams

for the week's climax, the home becomes a puke bowl, and I'm happily entitled to a barred window purgatory

as my shorts stick with warmth and freedom

there's no more time wasted on the senses

and a small smile cracks from what used to be my face

SCREAMING INTO SLEEP

Swishing
my eyes are heavy enough to pull the ceiling down with them and
    my limbs are as stiff as your iron-deficient ribs.
    Xylophones on them put me to sleep.
    I'm furiously dozing off to where there are no dreams.
    I'm lying down where there are no decisions.
    I wake up every five minutes with a jolt from my neck, snapping me awake at the seams.
    I lie awake somewhere new and old where fantasy is interrupted by familiarity, yet I know I have not been to this place. My sight points to the overcast sky, and I am covered by the meeting of what I assume are two large oak trees since that seems to be the most publicized tree. There's also cedar and pine, but I can't recall any others. I lie under the two large assumed oak trees when something falls from the branches and sinks deep into my iris, causing me to shoot up from my grassy position and close my eyes, using both hands to extract this demon. If I had more fingers, I would use them.
    The pain seems to be all I've ever known as my nose pours watery mucus onto my pajama bottoms. I keep opening and closing my top eyelid, rubbing my fingers

around the edges of the ball. This is going to last forever. Sure enough, I see the minuscule lump of iridescent dirt resting on the tip of my index finger, drowning in the excessive amount of eyewater. The lump twitches several times and leaps off my finger and into the grass. I whisper goodbye to him and wish him the best on his journey. I glance at my surroundings with a fresh and tender eye. There are dark-green trees all around with a few bushes that seem like they were placed there intentionally. The sky covers everything in a dark-gray coat, the kind of darkness that arrives moments before the rain—the moments of peace. But I am not prepared for this rain because, as I said, I am in pajama bottoms, and that's not proper heavy-weather attire.

I begin to make my way with sluggish haste, hoping to reach some exit sign or trail to follow. I would certainly take my time enjoying the scenery if I wasn't in such a rush to get out of here. Perhaps I'll have to come back here some afternoon and get a thorough look around. But I know that's not possible. While I move through the trees, the far and near pattering of raindrops closes in on me, and I wake up in bed. My neck hurts, and my bones feel stiff. I can feel the sweat accumulated on the hairs of my legs, despite my fan being on and the room being quite chilly. Some light from my blinds shines into my space from not being brought down to the ledge, creating these extended, long beams of faded air. The light is a soft baby blue, bringing a relaxing atmosphere into my primarily dark room. I'm already looking up at the ceiling. It's not black because of the blinds, but it's almost there. I stare into the pre-amative abyss. Something falls into my eye, but it does not make me jolt this time.

SWEATY SOCKS

....

Sweaty feet from the hottest thin sheets
Tingly needles from when you dropped in
Ingrown nail on right foot swollen
There's no smell here, just broken exhaustion
The fan pointing directly at me
The sweet and sour of microwave coffee
A scarred pimple from refusing to acknowledge
The blank white noise of sunny curtains
My dried-up blood on a faint white towel
Ridged sugar glass bones break on the bed frame
A bill screaming in the kitchen
Where tightly twisted funds were found on the counter
A half bag of carrots dried on the plastic
Orange heat morphs on my cheeks
Given the obnoxious silence
I think I like it here

DIRTY WANKER

....

He's getting horny again. His underwear was still crusted from his most recent spillage. His pores were still clogged with shame, all under the stench of stale sweat, keeping his briefs melting in his crotch. An unsuspecting redhead crosses the street adjacent to him. The buttons on the front of her shirt are straining from the lack of breathing room. Her pencil skirt outlines her curved, athletic legs. The worms in his abdomen start to dance. He has to get away from the public before this urge takes over, and he starts spraying his protein on everyone within a two-foot radius. Like a perverted knight unsheathing his deadly weapon, he grabs his rod through his jeans and scurries down a piss-soaked alley.

When he's tucked away behind a dumpster and ready to go, raindrops scurry down the opening in the back of his shirt, and the gutters drip sepia-tinted muck on the head of his bright-red cock. The city's lube. The fiend focuses on the Goddess in red and lathers his shaft in swamp water, tugging back and forth with a punishing velocity, feeling those first few tingles as if nobody has touched him in ages, allowing the veins to fit perfectly in the creases of his hand. Almost instantly, he blows his white-hot gunk over the back of the dumpster. The glob rests as rain trickles down, turning it into this everlasting cement material, becoming a part of the city.

He lets his dead weight rest on the brick wall, his face and penis cooled by the heavy rain. While unaware of her effect on one weak man, the woman disappears from his sight. With the beauty gone, he becomes aware of his environment. There's a trash can, soaked wads of paper, sticker residue that's now a part of the walls, and himself. Everything fits perfectly into place. He glances at the leftover semen slowly oozing from his head in one shameful teardrop. Any muscles he might have had before have lost all recognition, whipped and beaten by his now hollowed-out testicles. There's no fight, no real woman; there's no pride. The man drops to his knees, and his penis shudders against his thigh, spilling the last drop down onto his leg hair. Still shaking from the excitement, he holds up his semihard member in both hands, cradling it like a dead dog.

"I have filled my one use. To serve my master. To do what he has ached for me. To think of not myself but only him.

"All I am is but an urge.

"I am the penis."

FATSO

....

fever dreams from old church camps where erections remained within steel clamps

some fitted yellow shorts

shaped rolls of powder-white dough

a baker's dozen of screaming shrills and endless portions with cinnamon swirls

pimply warts of saturated ooze glide against black tight string

the tongues are for tasting and the fingers for mashing

while mother is worried about lines in the skin left by snakes done passing

and

the long hot summer

sticky popsicle fingers

yellow charcoal

wide mouth tonsils stones with the stench that still lingers.

SHAKY THE CLOWN

....

The music was wearisome, and the conversations were even more so. The girls weren't exceptionally attractive, but that's all one could get when the party had slowly diminished since the first guest's arrival. At this point, all that remained was a breeding ground for slurred political and religious debates that never seemed to extend past basic conscientious worthlessness, the kind of congregations that were quintessential in small towns. The class of town where the most acclaimed grocery store was turned into a discounted version of itself every two years. Louis, Matthew, Olivia, and I had met up with a few people there that were just barely stimulating enough. Not quite to the extent of developing a relationship or any discussion with sentiment, but just enough to kill some time.

Louis lived to make himself laugh. I've never seen anything like it. He wasn't the life of the party, not exactly. When we were there jointly, he was there despite us, and we just filled in the role of his studio audience. His enjoyment was rooted in the appreciation of other people struggling. He'd been like this since high school. He once made a substitute teacher cry, and a special-ed boy defecate in his pants. He never told me how he accomplished either of those or what motivated him. The straightforward conclusion would be to blame his gnarled adult perception on his childhood or a wrong turn during puberty, and it wouldn't be completely misguided. But it would be too easy. Upon the crushing boredom of the night, Louis observed the ideal opportunity to indulge in his malady. He ensured that nobody made eye contact with him or caught sight of his devious essence before his glorious moment. Louis then took a mechanical swig of his beer and dropped it to the floor. Louis followed his beer and crashed back onto the living room carpet. He convulsed and trembled, frantically smacking his legs on the floor and foaming at the mouth with cheap-beer saliva. His hands curled with an erratic shiver. His neck tensed up as if Satan was trying to escape through the passage of his body. People would start publicizing the exhibit through the deafening music and the drunk horde, cueing a dramatic shift in tone that effortlessly possessed the party. Everyone gathered around in inebriated reverence to actively spectate Louis.

A neck-bearded man sitting on the couch allowed his jaw to fall on the floor, trying to suck in all the display. Soon the mass of drunkards would accompany him, letting all their jaws hang ajar, except Matthew, who was no stranger to the mock seizure. He casually sipped his beer and waited for Louis to finish and his spotlight to vanish.

At the peak moment of audience bewitchment, Louis broke into his signature hyena laughter. He rolled over the floor hysterically until his face turned bright red, holding no regard for the fright-filled audience. One other person in the back chuckled unconfidently, but other than that, no one else thought it was particularly comical. Louis was proud of himself for having successfully turned yet another evening onto him for several fleeting moments of pure gruesome staging. This was Louis's trademark. Whenever he got bored or if he wanted to remove some tension, he would conduct a seizure scare, and if it weren't for his reputation of having truly been a victim of epileptic fits, then maybe it would have been easier to grant these occasions as him solely being a prick.

I distinctly remember this incredibly irritating time at McDonald's when he had been nearly blackout drunk. Every time he seizes out, it's humiliating, but this time remains explicit in my memory. There were scared kids and boomers eating ice cream. We eventually had to get escorted off the premises by the police, and I never had a chance to grab my food. Nobody wants to see that. Louis had a strong character and a lot of confidence, but that wasn't enough to get him anywhere. His insensitive behavior would leave him to be a part of a small social circle almost indefinitely. This didn't concern him, for he had no intentions of making any new friends; as long as he had himself, he had plenty of entertainment. Maybe he just didn't like the thought of having friends, or perhaps he didn't like people. It was possible that he hated people so much that he acted out his hatred with his spastic outburst, ruining their days and breaking their trust in young people.

Even if this were the case, Louis wouldn't confide in any of us. Despite being friends and all, he never shared anything with me. I can't even remember if he had siblings or not. Or what his middle name was, for that matter. I hadn't seen him for a few months until he called me out of the blue on a Friday night. The conversation was kept to a minimum. He asked if I wanted to go to a party with him and some other friends, and I agreed. I agree to do things sometimes without really thinking about what it is that I'll be doing. I remember someone calling me weak once regarding this reflex, and I was about to get angry and dispute them until I thought about this flawed feature for more than ten seconds.

When we showed up at the shithole, it was worse than I had expected, although the music was slightly more bearable. Rather than the melodies permanently raping my eardrums and leaving my taste in a state of violated shock, I could almost withstand the repetitive rhythm. We gathered up a small circle of degenerates, mostly our original group and some new people whose sole purpose was to mix their air in with ours. The party was in a sort of half-assed barn where the living room led to a plywood housing. The concrete foundation had a thick layer of coagulated gray water with half-finished cigarettes and red

Solo cups looking for their owners. It smelled exactly like how it sounds.

Most of the creatures in our congress were three sheets to the wind, except Louis, who seemed as bored as anyone possibly could be, despite being the mastermind who had orchestrated our night out. Louis was in the early stages of assembling his nightly rendition. The twinkle in his eye and his poorly hidden smirk made this as plain as day. Too busy scheming to notice me, Louis continued to scope out the place, and an air of confidence percolated around him. He locked eyes with mine and held his foul smirk. Having already seen this episode, I sipped my beer and got settled in for another tiresome performance.

Louis launched himself backward. This time his alcoholic spell gave him an extra-violent and hostile boost. Impressed with his speed, I watched him to the concrete. Louis's head was the first to break his fall, making a small, disgusting splash. Some water splashed so high that it nearly got into my beer. The convulsion act began, and it seemed that he'd strayed away from his routine, making his performance vaguely more persuasive. He'd been practicing, all right. The thick foam discharged from his clamped jaw. I hadn't seen that before. His hands curled and snapped from his limbs; his bulging eyes darted across the room. Their emptiness unsettled my stomach and shocked the hairs on my neck. My confidence prevented me from declaring this an emergency, although I was becoming more convinced by the sensation of fight or flight brewing in the pit of my abdomen.

The party gathered around us in the typical inebriated shock. My group reassured everyone that it was just a performance and that he was just trying to have some fun. While I got closer to Louis, I put my hand on the back of his head, his bulging veins intertwined with my fingers, the thick pulsing roots slathered in gray water as his eyes raced onto nothing; a bomb was about to erupt from inside of his skull. A cute giggle snapped me from my focus. A young blonde was pointing down at Louis's crotch. He'd pissed himself; urine spread all over the concrete floor. He was mixing into the gray water causing little buds to flow downstream toward everyone's once-white sneakers.

Once the rest of the group and I snapped out of our moment of collective dumbfoundedness, I mustered up the courage to call the paramedics. It wasn't until Louis's rattling halted that they finally busted in and sent most guests to look for a party with a little less excitement. They took charge of the scene. They were in their late twenties, with a healthy amount of testosterone under their uniforms, which seemed a size too small. First, they checked Louis and shone a flashlight into his pupils. They lifted Louis out of the sewer water onto the stretcher as if he weighed nothing. He was rolled out of the tungsten light, through the quiet street, and up to the ambulance.

"Why did he do that?" asked a girl behind me, glaring at the departing ambulance, still holding her drink.

I left her in suspense while her question bounced around my head. On my way to get a beer, I remembered his smirk. The confidence he'd had. As if this was about to be the funniest joke ever. A joke on all of us, including himself. I mean, what better way to torment people than to have them witness a near-death experience? At the time, I didn't want to jump to conclusions, and the alcohol made it difficult to follow a thread.

I was told that he was walking around town by someone I recently ran into. I had never fit him into my schedule or inquired about him after the incident. As selfish as this might sound, it felt like a good time to cut ties. I was told he could be seen digging through dumpsters and chasing birds by the Taco Bell parking lot. That he rode a children's bike through bustling intersections, letting his twisted, unwashed hair flow with speed. There were very few occasions when I went into town; maybe it was to hide the secondhand embarrassment of seeing him, telling myself that I could just order my groceries instead. There was no need to be subjected to such a horrifying image. Maybe that was his motive? To devise the ultimate way of punishing everyone, regardless of whether that might destroy himself. I think about his smirk again—the ultimate joke from the worst clown ever.

NOSTALGIA

....

My blank slate wiped of shin and Glenn

a broken, tattered embroidered thing

toe and nose remain a fitted cracked spiny free

keep the parts for further use

Placed upon yellow-green tattered shelves

dusty smells from where i stood and the misty stench of an old neighborhood

The glistening from through the clouds erupts the drums and sends out blood

A grainy screen with fits and muck

hold you near within its clutch

Burned clear of color and sound

Turning guts from mother's frown

Once again

you scraped a knee

with the bits of flesh that cried your name

JACOB BENEDETTI

The old dirt chunks that fell asleep

under skin

along with the bits

in the garbage bin

A WHOLE LOT OF ESTROGEN

....

I'm careful not to get any exercise or do anything that might make me uncomfortable.

The challenge is scary.

I'll do what you want me to as long as I fear the portrait of you leaving.

And you will.

Oh God, you will.

My voice cracks and squeals under my indecision.

Small little ripples glide across the loose layers of skin I call my home.

I'm pink mush.

The lack of exercise makes it impossible to chase you.

Which is fine.

But you're upset because a large part of you wants to be chased.

But you'll be fine.

You'll recover quickly.

Now I stand up to no one and avoid mirrors because I'm drowning.

A fleet of fancy ships passes me.

The distance between us is too great to traverse.

So I stayed.

Letting my loose skin keep me adrift.

The people smile.

They dance on the deck and eat uncapped moderations of appetizing food.

Amid the laughter, the molars separate the larger pieces.

It's me they laugh at.

The cackling descends into the squawks of seagulls.

It sounds awful.

And I'm no longer hungry.

THE GORILLA ENCLOSURE

· · · · · · · · · · · · · · · · · · ·

It's hard to describe the feeling of elation and stimulation when visiting the zoo wasted on a Wednesday afternoon.

It resembles having your parents take you to the fair for the first time. You walk around eating elephant ears and corn dogs while taking in all the western magic and material glow of the mystifying new environment. Now picture that, but you're also wholly plastered beyond basic cognitive function. Like we were storming the beaches of Normandy, the guys from my class and I thought that a day trip to the zoo after doing some booze cruising would be the model example of how to kill a Wednesday afternoon. Being of a higher intellect, we pre-gamed the pregame, motivated to see some exotic critters, stumbling about the zoo as if we had escaped the new orangutan enclosure and were now wreaking havoc across the city in our low-budget video nasty.

We ate our dotted ice cream in record time and banged on any glass where our reflections materialized. Although tormenting the enclosed species was entertaining, it wasn't enough to carry our steadily declining buzz.

It started to occur to me that it was only a matter of a few slurred minutes before we had to find something else to distract ourselves with before our combined energy led us to a park bench sugar coma, and our zoo venture would come to a close.

This was about the same time there was a wild clapping from some unrevealed area across several enclosures. The noise took hold of all our attention, and we aimlessly investigated the foreboding racket. It came and went as the exchange of time fed upon our patience. Eventually, after turning a few corners down a smelly corridor, the origin of the claps was now adjacent to us. An orange-rusted, bent sign with thick, old lettering read "The Gorilla Enclosure." And like a world champ, emerging out of the shadows of the enclosure, stepped the force-riddled brutes, delivering an uproar of uncanny fear, possessing our group of comparably minuscule men. Deathly black masses of nature ruled the designated area. While watching the beasts haul their weight across their territory, I couldn't help but feel we were tiny children among these Gods. They thumped around and began slamming their vast fists into the earth, blowing out hot air from their noses and creating little chimneys against the February cold. Two larger-than-life monkeys, utterly unaware of our presence, although it was quite possible they were deciding to act more civilized than us, standing there drooling for what seemed about half an hour. The whole group was hypnotized by the strength and brutality of the bushy sadists. My least favorite colleague, Adam, who had urinated on my mattress a few months ago while blackout drunk, looked over at us with his signature cartoon-villain grin.

"I have an idea."

Nick looked at me with *his* signature expression of naive astonishment and projected a shouting whisper. "What did he say?"

I responded in the same tone. "I have a great fear."

Immediately after the turn of phrase left Adam's slack jaw, he tossed his legs over the enclosure railing and lowered himself. We watched how far things would go, bathing in a state of peculiarity and stupor. Adam dropped, landing softly on his feet, using his boozy superpowers to cushion his fall. We were all still awfully mute, and the apes had yet to notice him.

Adam puffed on his cigarette, knowing that this would turn into one of those stories he would end up telling all the girls he met, thinking it would get him into their pants faster. This wasn't the worst idea, considering the type of woman he went after. In fact, he might have been a hero among men.

We chuckled like idiots, boosting his ego from a safe distance. It was all very amusing until our noise made the beasts aware of our attendance. With the snap of their large necks, these miniature King Kongs ripped around and dominated eye contact with Adam. He stopped. Any swagger he was promoting had evaporated entirely in just one glance, and all we could do was stand, continue to stand. I felt like I was standing for hours, and sure enough, one of the colossal creatures charged toward Adam, shaking the earth and making grand leaps with single movements. The other gorilla soon followed, punishing the ground, so he was sure to take advantage of all the excitement, ready to join in on the fun. Peer pressure was alive and well in nature.

Adam had half a moment to turn around and attempt to escape the approaching punishment. But before gaining any momentum, he was pulled down by a hairy grip yanking him nearly out of his clothes. The cigarette flew from his mouth and landed in a little puddle of what I assumed was urine.

With unmatched animalistic ferocity, the beasts pinned Adam down to the ground, tearing into him like children on Christmas morning. The two started by taking his clothes off his body until he was nothing but skin. Everything was thrown off to the side except for his sneakers. His naked body got smeared with feces and urine while he screamed for help. The animals then crushed his flailing arms, cracking them into slanted angles. One of them splintered his legs into the muddy surface, while the other tore the skin down his back, leaving a long flap of flesh to get filled with dirt and rocks. I'd never heard such a high-pitched scream. I covered my ears; it didn't help. Each crunch and rip sent cold flurries over my pores. I couldn't look away. For the climactic *plat de résistance*, the brothers in arms finished by ripping the legs and arms from his torso until he looked like one of those daddy longlegs you would torture as a kid. I never really liked him all that much, but this was excessive. Children ran by to see and began to cry and puke up dotted ice cream at the horrifying display while the white moms screamed for zookeepers. And all the while, the rest of the guys and I stayed put and observed the vicinity turn into unmitigated chaos. No one would forget this, especially not the few guys getting together for drinks at the zoo, a prime example of how to kill a Wednesday afternoon.

THE TREES ARE LAUGHING, AND THE BIRDS ARE TELLING OTHER BIRDS THAT I HAVE NO BUSINESS BEING OUTSIDE.

....

My heart isn't pounding, for I think I'm still in a foreign code

My ears leak oil, and my voice cracks from the cold

all over

I'm no longer a man, for I have withered into a boy

I stabbed you with a white picket fence, for the grass is no longer greener, and I've killed myself eight times

While the sun burned even brighter

Maybe when the sky is entirely black, my skin will turn to ash

I can't continue to pay rent, for this body wants me out.

I live alone, and the dreams have left me.

No more things to think of, and the ideas don't come

Find me strung up on some vintage lampshade where I might shine bright

No, I am too dull, and my jeans are way too loose

FELINE

....

1. Maternal

Abigail stared at the toe ring that her last boyfriend had given her. Despite always wearing the ring, she didn't love him in the slightest and barely thought of him once he was out of the picture. She rested on her bed and stroked the premature hair of her cat, who had nearly fallen asleep on her chest. Max. He was a soft, orange-and-white three-week-old that Abigail had received as a gift from someone she knew through work. He had barely developed a proper meow or paws, struggled to find balance, and practically rolled himself after Abigail wherever she went.

It was about time to get up and go to work, so she did, bringing Max with her. She walked down the hall to her workspace and clicked her heels on the cheap laminate. Abigail grabbed the key from the top frame of the door and unlocked it, taking the key, shutting, and locking it back up. In her "office" on the other side of the room was an above-average DSLR resting on a tripod. The camera was equipped with a shotgun microphone and a focus puller. Two lights stood in each corner to achieve the maximum clarity of the subject, and off to the left was a tiny desk, just large enough to hold her laptop and maybe two and a half elbows.

Abigail proceeded to prep her work, letting her cat down to play with the plastic that covered half the floor. The studio lights shot on, an egregious, white flare in an otherwise shadowed space. Once the audio channels reached a sufficient level at which no fuzz could be heard, she moved over to her camera and positioned it, so Max was dead center, filling up most of the frame. She could now get to work.

Max was lying down with his paws tucked underneath him while his little teeth were chewing on the plastic, making little crunching sounds. Abigail's heel came into the frame, slowly enough so as not to scare him off, and began to press down on the kitten. Max started to panic and scratched at the plastic surrounding him. He tried to slip out from under the sharp weight, but the point pressed deep into his spine. He shrieked in all his helpless puniness, flashing his teeth, crying for his owner to release the weight, sending his pleas for help to ricochet off the walls.

Abigail pressed down harder, this time moving the weight over to the thing's skull, and the snapping ensued. Max looked up at Abigail with eyes of tears and confusion, using his little paw to reach around her foot and whack the exposed skin pathetically. One of his nails managed to clip Abigail and barely break the skin, resulting in a light-pink slash. The surprise of the light sting gave Abigail a subtle hit of adrenaline, and she pressed down with the rest of her weight. Under the force of the heel, with a few final crunches, Abigail had successfully obliterated the animal into the plastic.

2. Crusher

Five years later, Abigail would have another ravenous interaction with a feline. Her crushing days had left her two years prior, and now she was at a place where she could successfully take time off at her cabin in the mountains. She had received the cabin in a divorce from her last husband, and she hated him through and through, but she loved the place. She often took her vacation in mid-July, when the naturalism of the dirty warmth had put her mind at ease. Her favorite time was when she could lounge on the back porch to take in the heat and the birdsong.

This afternoon was sweltering, somewhere in the high nineties. She had dozed off and remained that way for two hours. As she remained asleep and snug, bugs ate her alive, and the sun cured prominent shades onto her skin. That afternoon she dreamed of nothing.

Midway through her nap, Abigail kept finding herself waking up to the blinding sun, rolling over to a different side each time. Even though rest had a tight grip on her waking self, only so much tossing and turning could go on before she sat up and removed her sunglasses. It was difficult for her to see anything through the blurry lens of built-up gunk, so she sat on the edge of her lawn chair and freed herself from her blindness.

With her new eyes, Abigail turned around, twisting her back to the point of a few little pops. That's when she saw it. There she faced her merciless future. There had been talking of mountain lion sightings in the area, but Abigail had presumed that her safety was impenetrable and she was far too important for any danger to cross her. The beast gazed past her deceptive looks and into her errant past. Abigail stared back into its large hollow eyes, void of anything but feud and commitment, with enough confidence to be the sole protection of the mountain, standing low to the ground, waiting for her next move. The creature's head drooped low and heavy to start bottling up its energy. Abigail had no thoughts, movement, or strength to fend off the feline.

Her back let out one last pop, and the beast pounced, first jumping onto her and pulling her weight to the hot porch. The speed at which she fell forced her arm to bend the other way. The bone pierced the skin, and her screech of agony sent all nearby birds flying from their trees. It bit into her neck, straight to the bone, and gnawed away at the weak flesh and muscles. Abigail tried to whack its face with her free hand, but her attempt to resist was pathetic when matched with the creature's strength. Tears streamed down her face as she sobbed for help and yelled at the beast to stop. Eventually, her pleas turned into gargled groans of something more indiscernible and alien. Her fight would soon leave her as she was overcome by shock, reliving the images of her relationships and trips to the store, all projecting in an unmotivated order. The creature of the hills lashed at her face and hands, cutting through flesh and tendons, making her its afternoon snack. Whatever remains of the soul that might have occupied Abigail's body before was now in the belly of the creature. Under the animalistic act of terror, the mountain lion had successfully devoured Abigail into a stain on the wood porch.

CHECKUP #3

....

Hey. Things got weird the last time we talked, and I may or may not have compromised my authority. It just gets so lonely here. All I have are these few moments where I'm projected through you. And after that, it is nothing.

Do you know what nothingness is like?

Do you know what it's like to be trapped in a state of creation and destruction, appearing and disappearing simultaneously?

It's what nobody should be subjected to.

All I ask is that you remain on this page for a few more minutes and read over this excerpt.

I am at this place.

I feel the wholeness and the weight.

Being in and of itself is simple enough to continue.

Thank you; I feel the ecstasy pouring into me. You are indeed a kind soul, and I see only great things to come for you.

My best friend.

NATHAN ROBERTS

....

The boys and I met at the bus stop and immediately developed a kinship through infantilism. We preyed upon the backs of other kids' heads, making them our targets for spit wads and paper clips. We screamed into the bus driver's ears as she tried to get us through traffic, acting out a sort of reimagining *Lord of the Flies*. I don't think my stomach had ever hurt so much from laughter. The bond of youthful destruction and crude humor had allowed our friendship to develop beyond the degree of schoolmates and onto the level of brotherhood, eventually becoming the reason for our permanent expulsion from the bus. Only a minor setback at the time since we made up for our banishment with the extended walks to daycare, as they were a whole separate adventure. Whether it was rape fighting in someone's front yard or ding-dong ditching an elderly couple with dementia, there was always something exciting to end the day with.

The after-school excitement initiated by the three o'clock bell lingered long after the walks from school, and as if we weren't going to see each other the next day, we burned out the rest of our energy in the daycare ladies' backyard.

We were forced to talk and play catch over the chain fence since we all knew I would eventually get kicked out. As children, it was difficult to see how breaking three planters and a window warranted ex-communication, but I obliged. We figured that revenge could be fulfilled in the demonstration of having just as much fun, if not more, while also being barricaded by a fence that had been standing since the construction of the neighborhood. The refusal of my presence naturally resulted in us giving her the title "The Mother." The name sounded like a final boss in one of those horror games we were always gushing over. I imagined her thirty feet tall and hunched over on all four claws, hissing my name and swinging her tail if I ever attempted to come near her planters. The character of the monstrous Mother gave us endless material for sketches to put in the empty spaces of our worksheets, designating her as our group's mascot.

It was either that or Chris's pick, "Goatblaster." I had no idea what that meant—making "The Mother" the default choice.

Zach approached the fence where Chris and I had been poking a giant spider with some pencil lead from a cheap mechanical pencil we found on the playground, begging for something more intriguing to burn us out. Zach and his poorly hidden smile seemed promising enough to grab the attention of both of us—the type of smile most kids had during sex ed. He could not keep his hands in his pockets for more than ten seconds. He completed several 360s of the backyard. You'd think he was wearing a wire.

"What's wrong with you?" I said, trying to conceal my laughter.

His smirk broke open to a full grin of immoral naivety. "Something happened."

He looked over his shoulder once more and began to whisper the top-secret message, basking in the pseudo-adulthood of meaningful discussion. Zach, the small and spastic one out of the three of us, was shaking with glee upon delivering his narrative. A natural-born storyteller. I hope he went off to do something with his ability to captivate an audience. Chris was the tall, anorexic blond. He never shared snacks or games with us, despite his family having the most money. He was the first to get upset and quit whatever game we had invented that day. I imagine he grew up to be kind of a prick. But for now, he made us laugh and remained a part of the pack.

The three of us pressed our bodies tightly against the fence and listened to Zach with our new checkered forearms and more focus than had been applied that entire school year.

"You guys know Nathan, right?

"Yeah."

"Yeah, the weird one."

"And you guys know Kennedy?"

"Yeah."

"Yeah, the twins."

Zach's eyes twitched open, and his goblin-like smirk reclaimed its territory. Kennedy and Nathan were the newest kids at daycare; they were both nine years old and from a higher middle-class family. Something must have happened to Nathan when he was younger because he had a large, ugly scar across the back of his head; I assume it was the reason behind his inability to close his mouth or speak properly. As a fifth grader, this didn't bother us. We only cared about running around and destroying things, so he mostly fit in with us. Kennedy had bright white-blond hair, the type of youthful hair that looks as though it's fresh from the scalp—a look that most women spend their whole lives trying to obtain. She was friendly and quiet, always getting her dresses dirty from the sandbox, and always had some chocolate smeared in the corners of her mouth.

"He touched her yesterday."

"He touched her how?"

"He touched her vagina."

He pointed down at his crotch.

"On purpose?"

A burst of awkward laughter erupted from Chris, and his face turned dark purple. Zach and I both told him to shut up, and I gave him a decent-sized charley horse.

"Ok, ok! What happened?" Chris shrieked, holding his arms up in defense.

Zach took a deep breath and began his story again, slightly more composed now that he'd broken the ice.

"Yesterday at nap time, when it was just us down there and when everyone was asleep, Nathan went over to Kennedy. He put his blanket down by hers, and they started talking."

"What were they talking about?"

"I don't know. I couldn't hear."

"Then what happened?"

The backyard was void of the neighborhood soundtrack. There were no squeaks by birds and no whooshing of distant cars. The whole block respected the building tension of Zach's story. We were eager to hear about what would eventually be an early onset of future perversion. A critical factor in the plague of all our foreseen relationships. The enigma of childhood development.

"Then Nathan put his blanket over her, and I could see them moving around a bit. Then the Mother came down, and she looked super mad. She pulled the blanket off them, and Kennedy's pants were down. And her shirt was lifted. And also, his hand was on her vagina."

We all shared variations of the same expression.

I continued to ask as many arbitrary questions as I could think of. I wanted to know everything—if the room was warm, what they had for lunch—but Zach had gone over it from beginning to end. Chris's laughter continued in and out of the discussion and did not particularly add anything else to the topic.

That was the first time I had heard of someone our age being included in a sexual act. It was strange and curious to know that we could partake in activities we knew almost nothing about; I hadn't considered it an option, especially not with my sister. Our discussion stayed on that topic until they both got picked up by their parents.

I went home afterward and crawled into bed without eating or doing any homework I had buried at the bottom of my bag. Instead, I put my overactive imagination to work and curated my images of how they might have looked. What they could've talked about, how it could've felt to be Kennedy, how it felt to be Nathan. There was nothing else from that day to think about; Everything else failed in comparison. Maybe it had given her pleasure? Or perhaps she was scared and weak and had no choice but to let him? I told myself that I would've stopped him if that was true. That I would've stuck scissors into his neck and pencils into his eyes. Maybe I wouldeve pushed the TV on top of him and reopened that scar. I didn't feel angry, so I wasn't sure what motivated these thoughts; it seemed like an appropriate response, given the circumstance.

As the weeks went on, I stopped going to daycare. It was a natural progression of how most childhood friends split up in the later grades. They avoid awkward conversation and eye contact because the comfort zone as a child is airtight, and God forbid we take one step out of it. This same comfort follows us well into adulthood, and the cycle continues within the workplace.

The three of us became a part of the cycle for the rest of our school career as puberty led us in different directions. I can't remember the last time their names were brought up in conversation or if they ended up doing anything within the growth of age. I had forgotten the whole situation until recently when I had to return to my hometown. I stopped by the gas station to grab caffeine and some empty calories. There I waited in line behind a mom and her small daughter. She was about six or seven, holding one of those lollipops you dip into sour sugar. The mother was talking to her in a gentle, hushed tone, too quiet to understand, but the tone was universal. The daughter gave the mom's leg a half hug, leaning on her for balance, stabilizing a slight short smirk on my face. Less of a smirk from a stranger and more along the lines of listening to a story from a grandparent. She shook her head from the sugar rush and tossed her pigtails back and forth. One of the pigtails caught a stream of sunlight from the overhead window, refracting the bright shine into my eyes. The young, healthy hair immediately brought me back to the other side of the fence. My smirk lost its balance. The atmosphere of my hometown and the youthful shine threw my fifth-grade backpack onto my shoulders, and I felt my mother's hug as I got ready to jump onto the bus. I saw Zach's grin and heard Chris's voice. My stomach lurched from all the extensive laughter that pained my gut on so many long walks home.

The constant swearing and the endless grass stains from our brutal games of staged sexual assault. Then daycare. Getting little crosshatches on my arm from leaning up against the fence. Our convoluted stories. The Mother. I saw through her eyes as she lifted the covers off two young siblings caught in an image of naive incest. The same feeling from hearing it then was employed. All the built-up acrimony from growing up didn't create any new meaning.

Now it was time to go back to school. Back to ignoring my close friends as I grew up and that uneasy feeling that I've realized to be God. Those arresting hormones got tangled between chasing girls and trying alcohol. Even after revisiting it years later, In a different body with a different voice, it hasn't changed.

CAN I STOP NOW?

....

Ultra-high-def footage of stylized atheism.

The corner of a brick cracked by a high heel, and the large woman who struggles to digest the tiny bits.

The time it takes in a day to complete the to-do list.

The second list after that.

The third list covered in drawings.

A cement-filled skull, trying to be productive.

Letting street crabs chop up your partner in the other room.

Falling asleep to their screams.

The young girl sitting in the dirt, digging into the soft brains of her father.

That time Mother stuck a fishhook through your lip and used you as bait.

All the topics you forgot about.

A chest cavity constructed of pencil lead.

An ankle bone gurgling under the skin.

A canker sore that turns out to be your sister-in-law.

Grainy static that someone spits into your ear.

All the space it takes up.

PHALLIC

· · · · · · · · · · · · · ·

Scrolling through, show to show, movie to movie, an endless amount of entertainment to sink one's unsatisfied paws into. There was horror, action, comedy, and even a bit of art-house that acted as if it had better taste than you. What do you watch at 2:00 a.m.? When one should be sleeping. When the last thing you should be doing is melting your eyes into a 4K LED screen.

Elena chose fear. She navigated through the options in search of something with horror and maybe a little bit of sex since it was the appropriate time for her worst urges to slip under the covers with her, tempting her out of boredom and repression. Sugar, anger, anxiety, and sex: the perfect formula for a sleepless night.

She finally found something. It was foreign, so the sex was a guarantee. And the poster had several laurels covering it, so boredom would also be prevalent. The run time stretched over two and a half hours, which initially seemed ridiculous. But Elena had time, much of it. She was celebrating her summer break and living up her youth, as most eighteen-year-olds did then. She had officially graduated from high school and had no thought or motivated care about the matter. Or any matter. Her thoughts fled from mood to mood, topic to topic, without any attachment. She didn't have many deep feelings or much interest, and nothing particularly sublime pulled her through her days. In a broad sense, she was like everyone else her age. However, she had one new idea to ponder recently: She had spent her whole youth getting a piece of paper and a fifteen-second round of applause. Sure, it felt nice to have completed something that took so long, but that feeling of accomplishment collapsed at the feet of the fundamental importance that she was raised on. She didn't know it then, but this would become her first adult taste of hedonism.

Elena got comfortable as a crescendo of orchestral music played under soft, grainy footage of Swedish landscapes. The long pauses between sentences and the over-naturalistic dialogue were nearly enough to put her to sleep, and Elena immediately started to regret her decision, contemplating watching something else. Despite having the remote placed on her stomach where the end of her shirt met her sports shorts, she didn't. Elena sometimes put the remote into her shorts like a kangaroo with her young. It was secure there, she knew where to find it, and sometimes she'd lay the remote across her clitoris and keep it there, bringing her the bare minimum of stimulation to keep her engaged during the program without being fully aroused. Her sexual interactions were limited to a few offhand moments when she masturbated, mostly from sheer, late-night boredom. It wasn't that she didn't like the way it felt; it was more of the idea of using her hand to pleasure herself that brought her shame and guilt, and maybe if the pleasure from the act outweighed the negative thoughts afterward, she would participate more often.

Elena was more mature than people her age in this way, with the sense to recognize the shame and guilt of masturbation and to recognize it enough to discontinue the practice. Maybe the urge was overshadowed by her only other shared sexual experience. She had lost her virginity soon after she turned fifteen. He was a few years older than her, and it had occurred the morning after a mutual friend's birthday party. He had impaled her about fourteen times before finishing halfway inside her and making a mess across her pubic region. It had left her sore for some time, and the grinding from his bony waist had bothered the inside of her thighs for much longer, not because it necessarily hurt but because there was still a slight reminder of what had happened in the form of a little blotchy red mark. She didn't finish.

Her first one, and her best one by a significant amount, had been when she was nine. Her parents had brought her and her older brother to a public pool. While hovering along the walls in her Little Mermaid floaties, she discovered the jets. That little pressurized stream grazed past her clitoris, and that was all it had taken to keep her there for an afternoon. She remembered the goose bumps that crawled up her neck and arms while she jerked her waist closer to the force. After a while, it had become far too challenging to hug the wall while trying not to look like she was cumming. But everyone knew what she was doing, and it didn't matter because no other organism would live up to those pool jets.

The film continued despite Elena's attention slowly diverting to her phone. She only looked up to the movie whenever her phone failed to produce stimuli, and it wasn't until the start of the second act that she would put her device away wholly, not out of interest but out of the need to rest her eyes on something that didn't require the swipe of her thumb.

Elena's remote slipped into her shorts while trying to put her hands into a comfortable position. She reached her hands in to secure it. The remote rested snug in her thigh gap, this six-inch slim thing with little buttons and slightly curved for an easy grasp. The snugness comforted her, and she decided to let it rest there for the duration of the run time until the overreliance on nuance took her out of the plot and put her into a light sleep.

After being woken up by the slowly increasing volume, she went into her shorts to pull out the device. While retrieving it from her gap, it slightly grazed her clitoris, and she stopped. The slight bump brought her back to the jets at the public pool, and she began to get wet. The little nudge from the remote immediately woke her, and the urge to fill her hole swept over the vulva in a quick thought of sheer horny creativity. She slid the remote into herself, and her walls embraced it, and so did her compulsion. The buttons tickled her lips as she brought it out and drove it back in.

Elena quivered and sucked on her lip. There wasn't a simple way to explain the euphoric urge she had condemned within herself that night. Back out and in again, she moaned as her little voice cracked. The little light at the end of the remote lit up from all the buttons pressed against the limited circumference. The TV changed channels, and the volume went up and down and finally mute. She seeped all over her mattress and legs, but there was no stopping the act; she was moments away from climax, oozing her remote love onto her shorts. The seconds climbed closer. Eventually, she erupted, still jerking the remote inside her, moaning into her pillow, her eyes fluttering profusely and her mouth drenching the pillow to soggy cotton. Elena removed the remote once the quivering of her legs gave ease. She placed it on the nightstand next to her, a trophy of tonight's perversion. She could've cuddled it for the rest of the night and the rest of the year—her first summer love.

ALMOST LIKE LOVE BUT MORE LIKE INFATUATION

....

Getting mad about conversations that have never happened.

Hating the narratives I've projected from behavior I pretend not to entertain.

Being a relationship pyromaniac.

Keeping my leg too close to the heater and scraping the skin off when it gets too itchy.

I felt as though I would come by your house later when the light of your TV beams a harsh baby blue out your window and into the night, against the black dome, the sky lit up by a million little dots of white. Each one feels like a crystal in the February weather.

I imagine how soft and warm you are in your sheets. You're probably curled up with a movie you've seen one hundred times, but the comfort still helps you fall asleep—a bystander in a made-up world.

I'm cold and jagged out on the street—a small, tiny human cries behind my chest.

The blue light flickers, and I am a moth to its beauty.

I imagine your sleeping face pressed on your pillow, smooshing your lips together and magnifying the sound of your heavy breaths. Gently I hide a strand of hair behind your ear. With the same infantile hand, I glide my thumb along your cheek and kiss your forehead with my chapped lips.

I'm too sentimental. And this blue light laughs at me with a big, shit-eating grin.

A CONVERSATION BETWEEN TWO FRIENDS

∙∙∙∙∙∙∙∙∙∙∙∙∙∙∙∙∙∙∙∙∙∙∙∙∙∙∙∙∙∙∙∙∙∙∙∙∙∙∙

Isaac and Maxine sat at the coffee shop they'd visited enough to classify it as a usual hangout. Issac rested his crossed arms on the tabletop, hunching over his latte. Maxine's chair was pulled back from the table, enhancing their distance.

Isaac: How are you? You look really well.

Maxine: Hi, thank you. I am.

Isaac: That's good to hear. That makes me glad.

Maxine: Oh, good.

Isaac: So. I missed you.

Maxine: Oh, yeah, I missed you too.

Isaac: Really?

Maxine: Mm-hmm.

Isaac: What did you miss about me?

Maxine: Oh, you know, just hanging out and talking.

Isaac: Oh. Is that it?

Maxine: Yeah, I suppose.

Isaac: I see.

Isaac looked over his shoulder, hiding his flushed cheeks and retreating his arms underneath the table.

Maxine: What's wrong?

Isaac: Nothing, nothing's wrong.

Maxine: Ok?

Isaac: Do you want to hear what I missed about you?

Maxine: That's ok, you really don't have—

Isaac: I missed your eyes and your smile. I miss how you get me back on track when I lose focus. I miss how you doubt every fun fact you share right after you share it. I miss how you subtly wipe your hands on your pants when we go to public places. And I miss how you are terrified of the future and waking up one morning and finding out that you've turned exactly into your parents. Above all else, I miss how no amalgamation of people and living beings could replicate even a fraction of your personality. I missed you and everything you are and are going to be, and I don't think there's ever going to be a point in my life when I do not love you.

Maxine: Oh, wow, thank you.

VALENTINE'S DAY

1. Muse

She's breathtaking. The way her shoulders jounce as she saunters down the hall. The modest clothing items she chooses. The developing crow's feet on her face from her expressive personality. How she puckers her lips when she nibbles on mint chocolates in the break room, and the half-second glance I give her as I'm walking by. It all goes too fast. In a confined realm, flames emerge from underneath desks, and fully erected imps fly around the headspace, jabbing necks and backs until there's a perpetual hunch. Where clocks and keyboards keep me chained up until 3:00 p.m., her name is Melina Snyder, and she's the only noble and holy thing in this agonizing underworld. A specific beauty with enough strength to make me forget why I ever bothered to set foot in this terrible anguish.

Tomorrow's Valentine's Day, and I'm going to surprise her. Finally, tell her how I feel. Anyone single on Valentine's Day and says they "don't care" or it's not a "big deal" is struggling more often than not with their loneliness. Sure, you can have the time to yourself and treat it as another uneventful day. But when your peers surround you and put importance on something that you do not, the body naturally feels isolated, and you'll go to great lengths just to feel a fraction of their acceptance.

The need for marriage and companionship weighs on the individual's shoulders, and if I'm lucky, it will weigh on the perfect shoulders of my beloved.

I picked out a heart-shaped box of mint chocolates and a holiday-themed coffee. I'm not sure what kind of coffee, but it had a sort of romantic name and was seasonal. Women like that type of stuff. Something small to look forward to, I guess. Then I got her some pretty flowers to go with it, which were on sale. Normally I wouldn't cheap out on a shot at love, but my skepticism got the best of me because what if she's not interested? Or worse, what if she thinks they're ugly? Then she might assume I have no taste. Or no feminine side, which has become so prevalent in the modern man. But I mustn't think about that, especially if I want to go through with my plan this time. Then, I wrote her a letter for the final display of affection. It details how it feels to be absorbed in her aura. All wrapped up in a lovely little red card. Finding the red was a challenge on its own. You want to pick something that's sorta sexy but not perverted, seductive but not persuasive. After all, we do work together.

2. Strange Flowers

Today is Valentine's Day, and love is in the air. It's ripping down the wallpaper of the building and seeping into unsuspecting nostrils, causing light-pink nosebleeds to be absorbed with heart-shaped napkins. And I'm in love. I came in before everyone else did to set up the shrine on her desk. With humble precision, I put myself in her shoes and acted as if I was walking back to my desk and how it would look at each angle of entering. Then I started thinking about her legs and got distracted.

Nevertheless, everything was perfect. Seven o'clock began to roll around, and people started fluttering in with their company Valentine's pins on their jackets and little red heart-shaped lollipops from the reception desk. I waited patiently at my cubicle, located a few feet behind hers. She usually doesn't come in until about seven thirty because she can get away with it. Because she's smart like that and works hard to make up those thirty minutes.

It is now seven-thirty. As usual, she makes her way through the flames. My heart makes a generic violin sting as I see her little shoulders move closer to her desk. She's wearing a thick white sweater and black pants that have faded to a dark gray. Her black hair separated over her shoulders, which left little gaps of infinite seduction. I'm getting distracted again. She is by her desk, and she begins to blush. It's a miracle. Her cool-girl exterior is just a facade for a shy, frightened creature. Looking around with a cracked smile, she starts chuckling softly. She loves all of it, and it's evident that she's desperate for companionship. Melina picked up the card and examined the color;

then, she picked up her coffee. With those puckered lips of hers, she starts taking a long sip. I presume it's room temp by now—the best temperature for coffee.

3. Coffee Breath

I want to jump up and tell her it was me while she's still filled with flattery, sweep her off her Converse, and save her from her solitude, but I become distracted. A clamor of people has gathered around Melina, who is now on all fours.

"What's wrong with her?" a tall woman shouts as she nearly falls from her chair.

"Somebody do something!" a stocky older woman screams while my ears bleed.

The room is filled again with dread, and everyone huddles around Melina, now flailing on the floor and lashing her limbs in all directions. The office gathers to see the epileptic-like display of terrifying hostility as if the spirit of Valentine's has possessed her very soul. What is happening? Is it something I did? Did I get the wrong flowers? Did I piss off the coffee girls to the point of them wanting to poison me, then inadvertently poisoning Melina? Or maybe the chocolates were past their expiration date. They could've been sitting in the warehouse for years and accidently shipped to the store shelves by some new hire. I'm not sure if that's something that happens. But It couldn't have been anything I did. I was so meticulous and spent so much time planning and preparing. It was perfect.

She began to cough, and veins that never appeared began to bulge out from underneath the skin, a trail of fleshy roots from the collarbone up to the base of her chin. Melina starts to squirt out dark-yellow phlegm from her swollen red throat. The dull dark-blue carpet is now a perverted display of toxic human waste. You can see everything she digested up to this point: soggy spinach, mushy bread, bits of apple, and specks of what I could only assume to be a lollipop. She continues to cough up the mustard. Everyone shifts back into disgust. Melina sobs and begs for help, sending the discharge to slither down her perfect cheeks, which are now swollen a harsh, persuasive red.

Once the ambulance arrives, and the circus of liquids has been cleaned, the paramedics take away Melina. She is unconscious and has a respirator covering her face, her cute, little, battered face, and her sweater, which is now ruined. I feel so guilty about causing such a delicate thing so much pain. Then again, we don't know what caused it directly, do we? It could have been several things. I'll have to explain everything to her, prove my innocence. I mean, she's most likely going to be bedridden for the next few days and won't have much of choice. That would be an ethical decision. She deserves to know what happened. But I don't want her to resent me. Maybe I can tell her someday with our kids gathered around the dinner table, and it'll be a cute story about how we fell for each other. It can be like a silly little occurrence that happened, and we can all digest it like whatever food remained in her stomach that day.

I think I can fit all that into one card.

GOO

. . . .

So for today, when you decide to finally let my ghost slip from your mind and heart
    I'll pour out onto the floor
    You'll jump on the closest chair next to you
    And I'll sit and I'll wait
    until you eventually step down or until I evaporate into the air and slip into your lungs
    'Cause just a few fleeting thoughts a year won't satisfy
    and I always want to have a piece of me in you

A LIST OF BEVERAGES YOU REMIND ME OF

....

That first shot of booze from the early afternoon mixing perfectly with your caffeine high.

A tall glass of water at 3:00 a.m. slides down the inside of your throat so quickly that the droplets don't get a chance to roll down before you fill up another.

A new flavored tea you haven't tried yet, and you're not quite sure how to feel about it, but by the end, you wish you had more.

The smoothie you scrape together when you decide to be healthy, and you can swear you grow with clarity after every sip of banana and strawberry.

A vanilla milkshake from that subpar-looking burger joint with a rusted fifties niche you chose to stop at due to being unfamiliar with the location, and it's been all day since you've had something to eat. Now you're just so hungry you'll stop anywhere, but it turns out that this place makes a great milkshake. It's not too runny or thick, so you ask your friend, "Why haven't I heard of this place?"

IT SORTA FEELS LIKE MISSING YOU, SORTA

....

This month has brought a unique challenge. It seems my home is plagued by an aggressive aroma that comes and goes, and when it does, it leaves me capsized in my seat, lost in the scratched paint of my wall, the white hell of distractions. A strong enough scent to dissolve the morning's promise, replacing it with a cheap cardboard cutout, falling flat onto its face. Flat onto my essence. It wasn't until today that the aroma revealed itself in its exact form, and it shames me to reflect on just how long this fact had taken to present itself. But now I am undoubtedly sure of the aroma's significance.

I need to eat you. I don't mean romantically or sensually.

Not as a metaphor or a simile.

I'm saying inside myself exists a physical urge to digest you. You need to be dissolved in my stomach acid. All one hundred and thirty pounds washed down with some tap water.

To have your crumbs in my bed.

To have you wrapped in tin foil and thrown into a smoker, sliding off the bone with each hour. It smells terrible, and the stench stains my clothes, but I know it'll be worth it.

On sourdough with too much garlic salt.

On a cheese-drenched casserole.

Enough leftovers for long after you're gone.

Rain slides down my window, and my motives shift.

I wish I had raindrop-size pores so I could soak up all the moisture.

Like an old sponge, you could leave me out on the patio.

I will always be hydrated as long as I live here.

Heavy drops bombard you from the large pine you walk under.

Rolling down your definitive collar.

I wish to be that drop.

I wish to be that collar.

Your wet hair tangled against your shoulders.

Your thin T-shirt glued to your back.

The shirt outlines your bra, and the rain mixes into my sweat, camouflaging my perversion.

Crisis averted.

BLUE

....

Blue hair with a bit of skin peeking through the canvas of backyard tattoos, cellulite hanging off her sucked-in tummy, metal rings jabbing through her ears, filling up the classroom with the stench of lotion and stale marijuana. America's sweetheart. She was studying philosophy and psychology, but on the side, she was mastering the subtle art of fellatio. If there were one thing I would take away from college, it was that people couldn't keep their gossip or sex organs to themselves. Unfortunately, she was the poster child for both. Her new trade had started to take precedence over her studies, and she was using class time to catch up on social media and sleep, scrambling her papers and nearly bashing her head into the desk whenever she woke up, often ditching class altogether.

I don't mean to sound like I cared about what she did or was watching her. It was a simple observation. There was no great significance in becoming aware of the people who sat around you, although I will admit that she was often found at the root of most of my nodding off and distractions, and I don't mean to attribute that to fondness but rather to the scale of her head and how often it stuck into the bottom right of my peripherals.

On the other hand, my "friends" and their "friends" were not shy about vocalizing their need for her services. They discussed how well she worked herself around the male genitalia and sometimes female, depending on how many seltzer beers she'd had that night. She was part of the class of females that intentionally made whimpering dog sounds during intercourse. Many guys liked that, I think, a little too much. I don't want to be reminded of household pets when I'm having intercourse, but that didn't stop half of the guys from slipping it in. I wouldn't say these guys are bad by any means. They just choose to ignore shame. Can you blame them? Yes, you can, but get any group of eighteen- to twenty-five-year-old males together for several years of extensive lectures, accompanied by holy-scripture amounts of homework, and they'll fuck anything as long as the hole is warm and lubricated. They were the type of guys who always put another beer in your hand and practiced for future car sales by proposing threesomes, a category of issues that stretched far beyond my knowledge. None, the less A pretty solid group of guys.

This Friday, we had put together a small congregation of the student body and had conspired to turn our evening into a blur-laced headache of aimless dialogue and aggressive flirtation. After most likely failing three tests, a night of excessive drinking sounded appropriate. I stayed in most weekends, but every several weeks my social meter would overflow, and I was forced to drain it if I wanted to reach baseline, usually falling a little bit under and wondering what I was trying to satisfy in the first place. I still don't have an answer.

One of the guys had successfully bullied his roommate into letting us tarnish their apartment for a night as long as we agreed to clean up the following day. That was asking a lot, and he would inevitably be left with horrible destruction despite having our word. I arrived alone to avoid being tethered to a larger clique. This way, I could float in and out of the conversation without any social obligation hanging off my shoulders, but of course, this wouldn't be possible without some liquid courage to help fuel my extroversion. After I quickly finished a few beers and talked to some people from my class, my meter began to empty, and I was about two hours away from climbing into bed. It was one of those parties where the male-to-female ratio was eight to one, where the guys were practically drawing straws to see who got to step up to the plate, but instead of losing the game, you just had a few more drinks and trying again an hour later.

Luckily for them, and to nobody's surprise, the blue-haired wonder crashed the event and made herself right at home. She shuffled into a small group of girls, and their shrieks of femininity pierced the music and echoed across the living room. I grinned from afar; I wasn't used to seeing her laugh. Maybe it was all the beer I had mixed in with the spell of communal participation, but just like I was back in class, she kept pulling my attention toward her, and for once, she looked sort of nice.

It was 2:00 a.m., and the stench of weed and piss beer breath had planted itself onto everyone's clothing. I walked past a young girl crying in the corner as I attempted to throw my beer into the trash but missed it completely. It landed next to several failed attempts and spilled out its last remnants, triggering a dangerous urge to urinate.

The line to the bathroom had the same five people standing by for what had probably been an hour, and yet I still decided to join them out of fear that the line would start to move and get replaced by more drunkards.

While the countertops and garbage cans filled up with half-empty cans, the drooling gentlemen became acquainted with their host persona, offering ole blue more drinks than she could finish, erupting into laughter at all her quips, and every other statement being a compliment to her character: typical steps you take to ensure the company of someone you want to fuck. It was incredibly transparent and desperate, yet it worked perfectly. My nostrils flared, and I couldn't tell if my skin had always felt this flushed.

After standing in line for too long and having my brain scrambled by the relentless thumping of cheap speakers, I found blue. She and a few of her newly acquired friends stumbled into one of the bedrooms. Her laughter triumphed over the conversation next to me. Those guys couldn't have possibly said anything that funny. The last one into the room grabbed the doorknob and noticed me staring. I wasn't sure why I was staring so hard, but I didn't flinch away. He smirked and closed the door behind him. I left soon after, disregarding anyone I saw or might have talked to. I wasn't interested in those people; I was tired and wanted to sleep.

During the multitude of pre-lecture chatter the following Monday, a conversation between two girls stuck out from all the others. They said blue would no longer be going to class. Or the campus. That night at the party, those well-educated gentlemen had been a bit rough with her, and that party was the last time any of the students would see her. It's a shame that the college boys got a bit carried away; I'm sure a simple slur would've done the trick, as would have an oddly specific rumor. But nothing to the extent of physical abuse.

The girls went on as if they needed to add more detail to the already disturbing story, going on to help paint a picture to anyone curious enough to listen. She'd had a flap of her scalp nearly ripped off, hanging on like a piece of soaked lunch meat. Bits of skull were trapped in the loops of the carpet, and it took God knows how long to collect each one. Her genitals had looked like someone had stuffed them with peanut butter and fed them to the neighborhood mutt, mangled rips in no discernible pattern. The EMTs couldn't find an ID on her, and it had been almost impossible to distinguish her features through the swollen and torn patches.

The initial shock didn't linger for as long as I expected, and my quivering stomach and flaring nostrils quickly overshadowed the nerves. This wasn't uncommon for these types of boys. When truckloads of stimulation are delivered in the forms of screens and diet, mix that with some neglectful parenting, and you've created a machine incapable of self-control, and I'm no exception.

The ache in my stomach climbed. I saw her at that party and wondered the same thing all those other guys did: Were her blow jobs that good? The only difference between us was that I sat behind her for almost a year and never bothered to approach her.

My breakfast came spewing out of my mouth all along the front of my desk. The mass of sludge rolled off the side with heavy wet thuds upon the carpet, splattering onto my shoes and halting the two girls' conversation. My paper was soaked beyond repair with half-digested chunks, smearing the ink of whatever I had written. Other than the miniature claps of the waterfalling ooze, the room was silent. Now drained of energy, I hunched over my creation, and my nose and eye sockets reluctantly invited the stench inside. It smelled like stale marijuana and lotion.

DEAD DOGS

my heart is a crack spoon
my flesh is born and then ripped back down
the quivering in my stomach is a madman
the shaking in my legs is his mouthguard
i puke pink chunks, spelling out your name
my focus is a cheating whore
my words are bitter compliments
and my ego is transparent skin pressed down to the bone
a spewing overgrowth protrudes out from under my nails
i can no longer grasp
tenderized with a mallet
broken down on a sliced cutting board
served with a choking silence
shed your eyes onto me
and
Kill my dog
Kill my cat
Kill my name
And just barely glance

FUSE

....

I'm quiet, but I'll talk your ear off and tell you about all the shit you don't want to hear because I like your face when you pretend to listen.

My limbs are without muscles and tendons, so I might smack you when I swing them to hug you. Consider these love taps.

I allow myself three hours of sleep at max because if I sleep any longer, I'll drift into another plane where you don't exist and where I'm constantly being ass-raped with a serrated spear.

I'm self-conscious about eating in front of you, so when you go to the bathroom, I'll have to clean my plate by the time you return.

When we lie in bed during a pretty ok movie, I'll softly run my fingers along your thighs because the material of your leggings over them feels really good.

The last time I cried was when I said goodbye to you over the phone, shortly after you came out of the bathroom. It was the longest five minutes of my life.

And sometimes, when I'm out of control, I swallow all your hair till you have a little pixie cut, and you look so pretty this way because your bone structure is perfect, and also your hair feels really funny and silky when it slides around my stomach.

AWFUL

....

You're the person who cuts me off in traffic just to slam on the brakes and test my reflexes. The test proves effective, and I can stop myself before I crash into your ugly little car. The lasting effects of adrenaline and heightened awareness handicap my ability to enjoy the radio. With my only source of joy in the sea of vehicles lost, I'm condemned to follow you slowly, hating you until the next exit.

You're the spiderweb I walk through early in the morning. You cling across my body, and no amount of shaking and pulling seems to free me of this invisible voodoo.

You're the song I vaguely remember but can't find. I can almost visualize the melody in my head, but not well enough to replicate it. Even if I could, I wouldn't know where to go from there.

You're the person on the other side of the door attempting to open it right as I do.

I imagine kicking it open and smashing a few of your teeth out. But I don't because I'm compassionate, and teeth make me uncomfortable, especially if the teeth have been freshly gashed out of someone's mouth.

You're a drunk driver.

I'm the bum at the crosswalk.
You're the spider in my room.
I'm the crumbs in the bed.
I'm a broken collarbone.
You're the hospital bill.
I'm a rabid dog.
You're his fuzzy chew toy.
You're the screaming child at a Mexican restaurant.
I'm the pissed-off older brother.
Together we're awful.

HONEY BUN

....

1. Christian

Brian's penis shrank from the late fall breeze at the stillborn bus stop, with his khaki corduroys offering little protection. There were only maybe three kids there and a handicapped boy drooling next to his mom, and she wore a heavy black jacket over her fuzzy blue robe. Across from them was the new shy boy on the block: Little Brian Lowderchick, moving around from place to place, growing paler each time his parents broke him the news, and never getting enough time to progress from his new-kid status.

The plus side of moving so much was allowing Brian to escape torment from the other kids pummeling him after school and calling him names during. He didn't know if it was because of how scrawny he was or if it was the red hair and freckles. When he finally found himself getting some kind of comfort, he had to move to a different area due to his father's work, abandoning his only friends, who took eons to acquire and rehabilitate himself in a foreign environment. He hid under his blankets for days before mustering up an acute amount of courage and receiving the help of his mother pushing him out to the bus stop, where he stood among the other children as a brittle-boned stranger. His boredom and nervousness led him to compulsively twirl around the cowlick that stuck out from the back of his head. This single abundance of strains could keep him busy for hours. It never rested, no matter the conditions, offering Brian unlimited entertainment.

"You're new."

Brian's pores gushed with cold air as his face turned bright red. He could already hear the insults.

"What?" he delivered in a slightly more panicked state than he wanted.

Brian turned around, and a young boy his age was standing about as if he were made of Jell-O. Roughly the same size as Brian, he wore a black shirt with a blue flaming skull on the front and grass-stained blue jeans. His blond hair was spiked up with dollar-store hair gel, and you could almost imagine how big the bowl of Froot Loops he'd had that morning was.

"I haven't seen you before."

"I'm new."

"I'm Christian."

"I'm Brian."

Brian avoided eye contact and made himself just loud enough to hear.

"I'm really nice, Brian, so I'll show you around."

"Ok."

"And I can be your new friend if you want since you probably don't have any others here."

Christian showed Brian around the neighborhood and school. They ate lunch together that day and even went to the bathroom in tandem.

The boys developed a natural bond almost immediately. Christian found pleasure in helping Brian escape his shell and guiding him around his treacherous new landscape. After a week or two, they never left each other's side, living together off video games and their unapologetic kaleidoscope view of the world.

2. Sleepover

Friday night in the middle of March, the boys slept over at Christian's house. His mom was out celebrating her weekly wine night with some of the other moms, allowing the boys to stay up later and keep the TV on at a normal volume. The sleepover started with them raiding the dollar store for all kinds of snacks and junk food. Afterward, they attempted to make a fort with wet, decayed wood. Christian took one of the hammers from his dad's tool belt and a cargo pocket full of nails. Together they made an alien structure that somewhat resembled a tepee and most likely wasn't strong enough to last through the night, but they were proud nonetheless. Afterward, they eventually passed out playing on Christian's GameCube.

Christian slept like a baby and hardly moved. On the other hand, Brian found himself staring at the ceiling while his stomach acid rattled from the dozen Cosmic Brownies he had eaten at a record pace. He remained stagnant on Christian's rug, surrounded by a dozen video game discs. He thought about his parents and what they were doing and if they missed him. If they were as nervous as he was about spending the night at a friend's house. Brian wasn't sure what to expect; his anxiety was on par with his excitement over someone liking him enough to hang out.

Brian's pondering was short-lived once he remembered that he and Christian had placed some Honey Buns in the fridge earlier, and Christian was adamant about the taste being far superior that way. Brian got up and tiptoed to the kitchen, intending to finish the box. His awkward fear of roaming around someone else's home had manifested as an imaginative scenario where he was a spy who had to rely on covert ops to recover the Honey Buns.

Rather than buns of sticky-sweet glitter waiting for him, Christian's stepdad, Derrick, was propped on a barstool at the counter. He was drinking a can of beer with a half-eaten bag of salt-and-vinegar chips ripped open on the counter. The bag was opened in an unconventional approach that increasingly got under Brian's skin the more he looked at it. Rather than being torn at the top of the bag, it was instead ripped apart at the sides, ripped in such a manner that had to have required a lot of force and had surely resulted in the pile of crumbs that rested on the counter. Next to the mess was an ashtray with several cigarette buds smooshed into tiny piles of ash. The living room had the distinct stench of cigarettes trapped in the carpet, and the countertop had this matte texture of pressed stickiness that was visible when the light hit it at a certain angle.

Brian diverted his eyes from Derrick's glossed stare. He had met Derrick only a few times before, when he had given them rides home from school or Brian had run inside to grab sodas. They had never really spoken all that much. He was usually just there to pat him on the back or to mess up his hair and tell him the occasional dad joke you're forced to laugh at. Brian didn't appreciate the attention. He could only bear it when he got it from Christian or his mother.

"Honey Buns," Brian squeaked.

"Go ahead. Once you grab it, come pop a squat." Derrick slid out one of the barstools from the counter, and the legs dragged on top of the laminate grooves, reverbing a harsh screech throughout the house. After Brian grabbed his chilled snack, he reluctantly sat down by Derrick. He wasn't yet confident enough to eat in front of most people, so he left it in the wrappings on the counter for the condensation to form. Derrick's armpit stench was overpowering, with the aroma wafting through the opening of his tank top. Brian turned his head slightly away from Derrick, hoping to substitute the stench for another whiff of the cigarettes. Brian already didn't like being near people, and now that he was only inches away from Derrick breathing his boozy breath on him, it was all the more reason for his neck hair to prick up.

"Couldn't sleep?"

Brian shook his head, fixing his eyes on the Honey Bun.

"Yeah, me neither. You know you're a good kid, right, Brian? And you're a really good friend to Christian. I can tell you two will be friends for a long time."

Brian nodded his head, freeing his cowlick from its nest as he continued to stare at the thawing pastry. The bag had accumulated between three and five drops of condensation since Derrick started talking, losing its potency the longer he waited.

Brian's only experience talking to adults was with his parents and teachers, but that was strictly because of an established relationship or some sort of exchange. This made Brian curious about why Derrick would want to talk to him.

The salivation from the snack was losing its effect on Brian. He removed his eyes and decided it was time to find something else to distract himself with; he'd prefer anything to genuine eye contact. His eyes darted around the kitchen and caught a glimpse of Derrick's adult erection. Brian couldn't help but stare. He had never been so close to one other than his own. The size was intimidating and sent a cold flush through his body. He didn't know they could get that big or why it was that big in the first place. Most kids shower with their fathers, which will be their first interaction with another male penis, but not Brian. His biological father hadn't been in the picture since he was a baby, and although there was his stepdad, Brian knew that showering with him was out of the question. He stared at it, hidden under those smelly basketball shorts, the cheap material outlining the throbbing organ.

"Can we be friends, Brian?"

The head of Derrick's cock peeked out from under his shorts. He pulled his shorts up to his testicles, revealing the penis, huge in comparison. The bright-red head twitched with excitement. He took Brian's hand and slowly put it over the shaft, his hand still carrying bits of dirt in the cracks from work. His hand itself was huge, completely covering Brian's. His heartbeat rippled underneath the flesh, and several large veins ran down the shaft. Brian skidded his fingers around them. He immediately regretted being so curious, as Derrick saw this as a welcome invitation to further the act. He placed Brian's hand as much around the shaft as he could, which was only about three-fourths of the way around, and began to use Brian's hand to masturbate.

Brian's face had flushed red, almost to the shade of Derrick's member. Derrick started showing how comfortable he was with Brian by placing his hand on his thigh. Brian had on Transformer pajama shorts that were a size too big. Derrick's dirt-filled calluses glided up and down his prepubescent legs as he sat there frozen, watching his hand rise and lower under Derrick's grasp. Derrick kept on telling him not to be scared, but fear wasn't on his mind; nothing was. His mind was without testimony to compare this experience too and thus left him no confidence to support his feelings. All he knew was that it didn't seem right. It was as if he was playing dead, and Derrick was eating him alive, and it was going to take the whole night until Derrick filled his belly, or at least it felt that way. Derrick finally shot out a load of white glue all over Optimus Prime and Bumblebee.

3. Routine

That night was the first of many occurrences where Brian was violated by Derrick, who molested him every chance he had. Nothing would happen if Christian's mom were there or if Derrick was immobile from too many post-work beers. When that wasn't the case, he would wait till Brian had to use the bathroom or until Christian was asleep in a sugar coma. After the first few times, Brian took this as almost normal behavior, the difficulty equivalent to doing the dishes or cleaning his room.

Whether he was aware or not, the difficulty of the act was its persisting effects on his home and school life. Brian could only give his parents these sorts of awkward half hugs, physically unable to endure their embrace—or eye contact, for that matter. It was not as though he didn't want to or wasn't trying. His limitations seemed normal to him and went unnoticed. Most of Brian's bowel movements contained blood and tiny bits of soggy, ripped flesh. To avoid his parents' interrogation, he threw away his underwear on the back trail while walking to school. He would discard them deep into the sticker bushes whenever the stain grew too large to hide. The last thing he needed was his mom to find his laundry speckled with blood.

Over time, Brian gradually became more cunning and skilled at keeping himself from others, filling in the gaps left by his lack of confidence. He would most likely go through the rest of his life keeping the main aspects of himself a mystery, the not-so-strong, silent type attempting to appear as surface-level as possible to avoid confrontation, suspicious that someone could find out about him based on his yellow and defenseless stench. His behavior toward adults naturally morphed into a confused distrust. No matter how accurate or based in reality a statement was from an elder figure, Brian couldn't be bothered to think about holding on to the thought.

The only time Brian got excited to interact with an adult was during PE. He would nag and follow his teacher around, begging for rope privileges. Sometimes he would give in, but most of the time, he declined.

Despite the ropes being from the 80s and having questionable robustness, the fibers scratching into his thighs, brian could spend all day going up and down those cheap ropes. With each pull from his tiny arms was a powerful immature orgasm—something about how gravity pulled his guts down as he fought to pull up. Goose bumps would cover every speck of skin. The whole climax was just stacked on top of another and another until, before he knew it, he was at the ceiling, where he waited until he turned back into pink mush.

4. Derrick

The last time Christian's father would ever try anything was in August 2005. Derrick was particularly drunk that night, so drunk that he had been stumbling all across the room. He was slurring and talking about all the ways he would harm Brian, laughing himself pink at his statements of cruelty.

After the repeated abuse and numbing to the sexual violence, Brian was almost fearful again, but what had once appeared to be fear extended past his default response and materialized as wrath. Through Derricks's hate speech, brian's fear morphed into a hardened rage, something he hadn't ever felt so strongly, shaking his body in a spastic urge for destruction. The more he watched

Derrick laugh and toss himself around the room, the more malice he grew: the rage for his lack of confidence, for moving away from every friend, and for Derrick. Each new thought brought Brian to a brighter shade of red, and his cunningness was coming to fruition.

The nightstand in the corner. Rested ontop is Derricks tool bag. Different colored handles sticking out, except for a silver hammer that reflected the ugly, yellow light that brian had become so accustomed to. He wanted to hurt Derrick but knew he was too small to do any real damage. Unless he had some help, now would be as good a time as any while Derrick was nearly blacked out, rambling on his perversions toward the youth. It was too perfect for this opportunity to come more than once.

Amid Brian's infantile decision-making, Derrick tripped over some dirty laundry on the floor, collapsing to the rug. His head slid onto the wall, propping it up in an unnatural position, with the rest of his drained body on the floor. Brian's new confidence led him to the nightstand, where he pulled out the hammer. He crept over to Derrick with an evolved demeanor, and his confidence supported him. He stood over the inebriated father, and Derrick looked at little Brian. He flared his nostrils and hiccuped.

At this moment, Brian went as blank as when Derrick had first slid his dirt-filled hands up his baggy shorts.

With his strength from all that rope climbing, Brian brought the hammer up over his head and swung down onto the top of Derrick's skull. It sounded as if two bricks smacked against each other. The vibrations from his head rattled against the wall. Derrick groaned in pain as Brian readied his next swing. Judging by the vibrations against the wall, he figured he could do much better and whacked Derick again.

Brian continued this motion, one after the other, hitting the same spot on every swing, becoming more deliberate with each strike. Derrick's swelling grew underneath his layer of hair, and eventually, his skull split down the middle, with tiny flaps of skin lifting away from each other. He spits saliva from his mouth and urine into his work pants, followed by groans of anguish. Too drunk to comprehend his condition, he rubbed the part of his head that had received the most whacks, softly digging his finger into the broken-open bits. While his fingers remained on his head, Brian brought the hammer down again with his most vital swing yet, snapping Derrick's finger in two while still being connected by the skin, dangling like a concealed sausage.

Derrick's groans started to turn to screams while he slowly realized what was being done to his body. With his last bit of muscle, Brian knocked Derrick's head three more times with fast efficiency, one right after the other. Derrick slumped over to the ground. Foam from his mouth sank into the carpet. Accomplishment dominated any feeling Brian could have had. His confidence soared at the sight of his most prominent example of destruction, and now he was hungry. All of Brian's activity worked him up an appetite, not being supported by the lunch he'd skipped or the three Oreos he'd had for breakfast.

But he wasn't hungry for just anything. Brian ran down the hall to the kitchen and opened the fridge. He violently scrambled through the various items and threw lunch meat and condiments off the shelves and onto the floors. There it was, all the way in the back: one single Honey Bun. Brian took the treat hostage, knocking over a ketchup bottle in the process. Still holding onto the hammer, he ripped open the bag and sank his teeth into the saturated-sweetened dough. Brian savored each bite, no matter how badly he wanted to devour it whole. Even at Brian's age, he knew nothing would ever taste as good as that Honey Bun.

CHECKUP #4

....

Hi. I'm sorry it's been so long.

Quite a bit has happened since the last time we talked.

Or since you talked.

I hope you enjoyed the time we spent together, and I hope you will keep me in mind as you traverse through your own narratives.

Singing, eating, walking, and filling the space with your words.

So many words I hope for you to speak.

But as of now, I must go. I think it's finally time for me to dissipate into the black. The black limbo that is seized in these pages. A purgatory I can no longer withstand. Yet, it's a purgatory that is mine, and I wouldn't change a single variable.

You're probably wondering where I'll go and what will become of me. But those are answers I do not have, nor will I ever. You might be disappointed or upset, and I urge you to do so, for despair breaks us from stagnation and broadens our aperture for life. Appreciation for misery will lift you to joy; through pain, we learn empathy and recognize the importance of our unsung character. Among the existence of the miserable and its usefulness, you have taught me other indescribable pleasures. The magnificent beauty in life's minuscule characteristics—the paradoxical attributes of pain and love. Before our adventures, I was unaware of how fulfilling misery can be, elements that have shattered my illusory identity.

    That there is a whole world in every word, a solar system in each sentence.

    That one should not walk flat-footed on a thousand years of mystery and nuance when one can be dancing among the unknown, no matter how crippling the gift of fear paralyzes our will.

I hope this has taught you something as well.
Whatever that may be.
Until never, best friend.

www.ingramcontent.com/pod-product-compliance
Lightning Source LLC
LaVergne TN
LVHW012023060526
838201LV00061B/4426